ANIMORPHS®

The Hidden

K.A. Applegate

AN
APPLE
PAPERBACK

SCHOLASTIC INC.
New York Toronto London Auckland Sydney
Mexico City New Delhi Hong Kong

Cover illustration by David B. Mattingly
Art Direction/Design by Karen Hudson/Ursula Albano

ISBN 0-439-10678-8

12 11 10 9 8 7 6 5 4 3 2 1   0 1 2 3 4 5 6/0

Printed in the U.S.A.
First Scholastic printing, March 2000

The author wishes to thank Laura Battyanyi Wiess
for her assistance in preparing this manuscript.

For Michael and Jake

The Hidden

CHAPTER 1

My name is Cassie.

And you wouldn't know it to look at me but I'm in the middle of a violent war to save Earth from an alien, parasitic species called the Yeerks.

Well, most of the time I am. Right now I was kneeling in the barn, waiting for an injured mouse's curiosity to get the better of him. And when it did, when he crept out from beneath the cage he'd scurried under, I was going to scoop him up and take a look at his crooked, back leg.

I guess that's just me. It's who I am. I don't like seeing an animal in pain if there's something I can do about it. And I usually am doing something about it, because my parents are vets and I

1

guess you could say I'm following in their foot-steps.

Except that in one way, I'm already way ahead of them.

I'm an Animorph. An animal morpher.

My friends and I were given the ability to acquire the DNA of other creatures and morph them. This power is the only real weapon we have in our fight to save humanity.

But it's more than that. For me, at least.

Every time I morph an animal, I experience the world as that animal does, sensing it, sharing its instincts. That's knowledge my parents will never have. And I'm not sure *not* having it is such a bad thing.

I mean, it's one thing knowing that a humpback whale can weigh thirty tons but it's a whole other story to actually weigh that much. To cruise the ocean with the certainty that you actually *are* that animal. The only way to really understand is to become that creature, and they can't teach that in vet school.

But this isn't just about becoming an animal. It isn't just about the morphing. See, we use our morphs to fight this war. To divert and battle the Yeerks. That's why Jake, our leader, doesn't like us using the morphs for our own purposes. I can't say I never have — there's nothing like frolicking as a sleek playful dolphin, and being a horse has certainly come in handy on occasion — but I like Jake a lot — okay, maybe I feel even stronger than "like" — and what he says makes sense, so I try not to do anything that would put us at risk.

But the risk isn't the worst of it. This is a war and people die. And using this power to destroy others is hard to get used to. But as much as I hate inflicting pain and sometimes death on the other Yeerk-infested species, I can't just sit back and allow their evil to consume us, the human race, too.

The Yeerks are like a disease, except they spread with malice and intent. A Yeerk will squirm into your ear canal, flatten out its blind, deaf, sluglike body, and weave into the crannies of your brain. Tap into your thoughts. See through your eyes, speak with your voice. You are a hostage, trapped inside yourself. Screaming for help but no one can hear you.

We call people infested by Yeerks Controllers, and there are more of them every day. Like I said, the Yeerks have taken over other species, too, and they're using some of them to wage this poisonous war on Earth.

We, the Animorphs, are the only active resistance. Me. My best friend Rachel. Jake. His friend Marco. Tobias, who stayed in his red-tailed hawk morph longer than the two-hour limit and now lives as a bird of prey. A *nothlit,* as Ax would say.

Ax is an *aristh,* an Andalite warrior-cadet, and it was his brother Elfangor who gave us the blue morphing cube before Visser Three murdered him, so that we could continue the battle.

That's pretty much it on our side. Well, unless you count the Chee, a nonviolent race of androids, who help us by spying on the Yeerks and infiltrating their cover organization called The Sharing. But when it comes right down to it, we're the only ones out there aggressively defending our species.

So you can see why I need to work with wounded animals. To help heal them. And in some way, I think they help heal me, too.

Movement.

A tiny, twitching nose poked out from under the cage.

The barn turned Wildlife Rehab Clinic was quiet today. We had only three patients and all were on the mend.

Their snuffling and scrabblings were familiar sounds.

But the distant, low-level drone thrumming through the air wasn't.

A chainsaw?

The buzzing grew louder. Sharper. Closer.

A low-flying plane?

The mouse zipped out. Stopped. Nose twitching.

THWOK! THWOK! THWOK!

The drone was deafening now.

The mouse tensed.

My hand flashed out and scooped it up.

"Nobody's going to hurt you," I said, but my voice was lost in the thundering noise. Something deep in the pit of my stomach stirred uneasily.

It didn't sound like a plane, it sounded like a . . .

I stuck my head out of the open barn doors in time to see a helicopter pass and continue out over the woods.

The droning faded.

I shrugged and turned to put the mouse in a cage and nearly ran into Erek who was standing behind me. Erek is one of the Chee.

"Whoa!" I said, startled. "I didn't see you come in."

Erek nodded. "Good. You weren't supposed to. And neither were the Controllers in the helicopter. We have a *major* problem, Cassie."

"Uh, I'm the only one here right now," I said, realizing I was still holding the mouse. I gently put it in an empty cage and then waited to hear the rest of Erek's news.

"I'll notify the others, but we have to move on this. The Yeerks have managed to repair the Helmacron ship and they've reactivated the sensors that locate morphing energy."

Oh, great. The Helmacrons. Again.

The Helmacrons are an exceptionally tiny, exceptionally annoying species with delusions of grandeur and egos the size of Montana. Unfortunately, they also have very advanced technology.

Erek continued, "The Yeerks are tracking morphing energy."

"But I haven't morphed —"

The blue box. The Escafil Device. It was hidden here in the barn.

"The ship's sensors aren't operating at full potential but the Yeerks have managed to hone in on a weak signal from somewhere in this area. That would be the energy from the morphing cube." Erek's voice was muted as the helicopter did another flyby. "They're making another pass. If we don't get that cube out of here —"

"I'll get it," I said, heading to the darkest section of the barn. I'd hidden the cube where it wouldn't be found by anyone who happened to be stumbling around, but I hadn't counted on the Yeerks being able to repair something so minuscule as the Helmacrons' damaged and abandoned ship. "But what good will it do to move the cube, Erek? Won't the Yeerks just target it again?"

"Yes. That's why you and the others have to keep it moving until the Helmacron ship can be destroyed," Erek said as the helicopter's shadow passed over us, blotting out the sunlight streaming in through the doors. "If that cube falls into Yeerk hands . . ."

"Don't even say it," I said, tucking the cube into the waistband of my jeans and pulling my dad's huge, old, college T-shirt down over it. "Okay, let's go —"

But Erek had vanished.

"Cassie?" my mother said, from the doorway. "I'm off to The Gardens. I have animal transports to oversee and —"

"I'll go with you!" I blurted, while giving the barn a quick once-over for Erek. Was he that bucket? That bale of hay? The Chee were extremely good with holograms.

The sunlight behind my mother shimmered and for an instant, Erek was Erek again and not a hologram of a brightly lit barn door.

I looked at my mom. "Let's get going."

CHAPTER 2

Have you ever had one of those horrible dreams where something is chasing you and no matter how fast you try to run, you're not getting anywhere?

Well, that's exactly how I felt driving to The Gardens with my mother.

The helicopter was buzzing back and forth over the woods. And we were getting nowhere fast because my mother was talking while she was driving, and when she does that, she always takes her foot off the gas pedal. She doesn't do it on purpose but it's still nerve-racking.

Speed up. Slow down. Speed up. Slooowwww dooowwwnnnn. . . .

BEEEEEEEPP!

"What's wrong with him?" my mother asked, scowling into her rearview mirror at the car behind us; it was crawling right up our butts. "The speed limit's forty-five on this road."

"Yeah, but you're only doing thirty, Mom," I said, gazing pointedly at the speedometer.

C'mon, Mom, hurry!

"Thirty?" my mother asked, pressing the gas pedal. The speedometer needle was on the rise. Sort of. "There. That's better."

But it wasn't better because the car behind us floored it, passed us on a double line, then cut right back in front of us and promptly slowed down.

"What are you doing!" my mother shouted, braking and glaring at the back of the driver's head.

"Mom, don't say anything," I warned, watching as the driver finally sped up.

"But he's driving erratically," my mother said, speeding up and then slamming on her brakes as he slowed down again. "What is he doing?!"

"Mom, stop! He can't hear you!" I said. "Just back off. It's either road rage or . . ."

Or a Controller sent to steal the blue box.

I looked up at the sky. The helicopter was the size of a horsefly in the distance. If it had pinpointed us, it wouldn't send just one Controller for the box. No way. Stealing it would be a major victory for the Yeerks and they'd send an army to do it, not one bald guy in a Ford Taurus.

". . . or he's a complete imbecile?" my mother snapped, but backed off enough for him to pull ahead. "I don't know what is going on around here today."

"You mean with all those helicopters?" I asked as casually as I could while keeping an eye on the car in front of us. It was on the move now and was pretty much history. "I thought maybe an animal had escaped from The Gardens or something."

"No, they would have called me," my mother said. "And I haven't heard any news bulletins about any hikers lost in the area, either." She smiled. "I guess it's just one of those days, huh?"

"I guess so."

By the time we pulled into The Gardens, my neck was cramped and my stomach was twisted. One from watching the helicopter, the other from sheer worry. What if Erek hadn't gotten word to everyone?

What if he had?

Wouldn't the Helmacron sensors pick up three kids and an Andalite in morph? Of course they would. Tobias would be okay, but was getting us all together really that great an idea?

The frantic fluttering in my stomach got worse.

I left my mother in the employee parking lot and headed into the park. I told her I was going to check out a few of the new animals and then grab a bus back home. I tried to look as normal as I could in my baggy, dirt-stained jeans with a blue morphing cube hidden beneath my T-shirt.

<Another bizarre fashion statement, huh, Cassie?>

Thought-speak. Rachel was here somewhere. Good. Even though I wasn't in morph and couldn't answer her, I felt better.

<She calls it cornfield casuals,> Marco smirked. <Bird poop-à-porter. We're in seagull morph, Cassie, so don't look up.>

<Erek told us about the Helmacron morphing sensors,> Jake said. <We're going to have to find a way to disable that ship. You have the blue box, right?>

I nodded slowly, paused by the American buffalo enclosure, and casually looked around — then up.

A red-tailed hawk circled high above me.

Two identical seagulls landed near the buffalo wallow. A third landed on a nearby Dumpster. A fourth strutted past, eyeing up a little girl eating french fries.

That one had to be Ax.

The kid giggled and threw him a fry.

He gobbled it down and screeched for another. And another.

<Hey, Ax-man, want to try and get a grip?> Marco quipped, swooping down and chasing Ax away from the kid.

<The clock's ticking here,> Jake said quietly but firmly.

I scanned the crowd, following one woman's gaze into the sky. Another helicopter had joined the first.

I glanced back at the woman, who didn't look surprised or even curious. Just sort of . . . eager.

She disappeared into the crowd.

The knot in my stomach was back with a vengeance.

The helicopters were circling closer and it wouldn't be long before they pinpointed a whole lot of morphing energy in one place.

I didn't know what to do. I couldn't communicate with anybody —

<Helicopters heading this way,> Tobias called down. <And there's a couple of guys in suits jogging toward Cassie.>

< Cassie, move,> Jake said tersely.

I stepped backward, away from the buffalo enclosure. Where? I mouthed silently.

<Anywhere! They're coming through the park, so head back into the employee area or some-

thing!> Jake shouted, taking off. <Everybody else, split up! We have to draw the sensors away from Cassie! Tobias, you stick with her since you're not in morph.>

<Cassie,> Tobias said. <They're closing in fast.>

And suddenly, I saw one of the guys in the suits.

I didn't run. I didn't want to attract attention.

I waited until he turned away.

Then bolted.

CHAPTER 3

<Nice,> Tobias said. <He didn't see you but the copters are still tracking you and feeding the ground guys info. Keep going.>

I did, my heart pounding in my ears. My all-too-human ears.

I was so helpless as a human. I had brains but no brawn. No claws, no fangs, no wings. Nothing to give me even the slightest advantage over the Yeerk-infested human-Controllers tracking me.

If only I could morph without attracting the sensors.

If only the others could distract the Controllers long enough for me to get away.

If only, if only!

Deal with the realities, Cassie. Keep going.

The alley finally led me to the loading area, where a couple of huge trucks were parked.

<Watch out! There are two guys on the other side of that big black delivery truck, Cassie! They're looking around, talking into radios. They're splitting up!> Tobias yelled. <Get out of there!>

Where was I supposed to go? I flattened myself up against a white transport truck, the only thing left between me and them.

And if one of the helicopters buzzed over now, they'd see two Controllers not ten feet away from a terrified, trapped-looking kid plastered up against a truck, with the sharp corner of the morphing cube poking up from beneath her grubby T-shirt.

They would know it was me they were hunting for.

This was it. There was no escape.

No way out!

I couldn't morph so I couldn't fight or fly.

I couldn't drop the cube and run because if the Yeerks got the cube, it would all be over.

My stomach pushed into my throat.

<They're coming around the truck, Cassie! Wait, there's a driver getting into the cab. Your

mother's making him sign something. The Controllers are at the back of the truck! If they look around the side —>

He didn't have to say anymore. I already knew what would happen. They'd see me. Grab me. My mother would get involved and then it was down to the Yeerk pool for both of us and total annihilation for my friends.

Trying not to hyperventilate, I inched along the truck toward the cab. At that moment, I didn't know what I was going to do, but I had to get farther away from the back of the truck.

Not that two or three feet would make that much of a difference, but it was all the space I had.

Something jabbed me in the back.

I flinched and glanced behind me.

A door handle.

There was a small, side entry door in the wall of the transport truck's bed.

"Chopper's picking up a reading from this area," one of the men behind the truck said. "If we find the Andalite bandits and the morphing technology, Visser Three will be extremely pleased. If we don't —"

"Don't even mention what'll happen if we don't," the other Controller said nervously. "The chopper pilot says the signal's strong in our radius. Let's just keep looking."

Panicking, I yanked on the door.

Nothing.

The truck started up. Idled.

It was going to pull away and leave me here, exposed.

I yanked again. Saw the pin. Pulled it out and pulled the door open, scrambled up into the back of the heavily fenced transport truck, and quietly closed the door behind me. Doubled over, panting, heart racing.

I had made it.

That's when something very large bellowed very loudly.

I shot up and staggered back against the wall.

There, looming in front of me, with its huge, broad head held low and its massive, curved horns, stood almost a ton of solid, muscled African Cape buffalo.

Aka the widow-maker.

CHAPTER 4

Several things happened at once.

The truck rumbled and jerked to life.

The Cape buffalo stumbled backward, bound by two ropes around its horns and two around its neck. The ropes were knotted into metal loops on the truck's walls.

The ropes were frayed and flimsy-looking compared to the buffalo's massive head. But then again, most people wouldn't have to worry about the ropes because they would never, ever get into a truck with a widow-maker.

"But the reading says the signal's honed in on this area!" someone shouted from outside.

"Yeah, but it's also picking up four other readings in four other directions!" someone else

18

said. "If you ask me, this is some kind of wild-goose chase."

"Don't let the visser hear you say that," the first man said uneasily. "He just pulled up."

The voices faded as the truck lurched forward, picking up speed.

<You're headed toward the back exit, Cassie,> Tobias was still around. Faint but around. Silence. <Uh-oh.>

Uh-oh what? I thought. I held still and watched the Cape buffalo watch me. Not a good feeling. Trust me.

It was hot and waves of the animal's thick, musky scent were nearly overpowering. Even for me. But the stench wasn't anything compared to the pure power in the broad, muscular body and the deadly threat of its massive horns.

The buffalo snorted, blowing a rush of hot, moist air out through its nostrils.

<They're going to stop you outside the gate, Cassie, at that stretch of road surrounded by woods.> Tobias was starting to sound a little frantic. <Visser Three's limo is right behind you and there's a bunch of other cars waiting around the bend.>

The buffalo snorted again. Tossed its head in a threatening, hooking movement, pulling the ropes taut.

The truck began to slow and lean into the bend.

19

The truck nose-dived, sending almost a ton of buffalo surging right at me. The ropes tightened as a rippling wall of muscle —

SNAP!

One of the ropes broke and pulled apart like a piece of thread.

I whipped left and flattened myself against the wall of the truck as the buffalo skidded forward and sideways, fighting the remaining restraints.

The buffalo bellowed again, thrashing in anger.

WHAP!

Another restraint. Gone.

The last two ropes were around the buffalo's neck. Somehow I figured they wouldn't be there for long.

It whipped its head around in a frenzy. The buffalo was going to break loose, and either trample or gore me to death. Impale me on those wicked, gleaming horns.

And then Visser Three would have the morphing cube.

There really was only one way out of this.

I inched sideways, watching the buffalo watch me. It was tense, just seconds from erupting again. I was shaking. I had to get past those horns but I knew it'd never let me get behind it where it couldn't see me.

The truck braked harder.

The buffalo stumbled forward, past me, to the ends of the remaining ropes.

Trembling, I laid my hand on the buffalo's thick hide, right at its midsection, and began to acquire it.

The buffalo gave one last thrash, then went into a kind of dreamy, semi-trancelike state. It happens to most animals when we acquire their DNA. Most, but not all.

"Hey, what's with the roadblock?" The shout came from the truck's cab.

The truck was barely creeping forward now.

In a minute it would be stopped and searched.

Would I have enough time?

I stripped down to my morphing outfit. Jammed my clothes out of sight behind one of the truck's wide, wooden slats. Laid the blue box on the floor of the truck and focused on the Cape buffalo's DNA.

Crrreeeaaaacccckkkk!

My skull split straight down the center and began to thicken, dragging my head down with the weight and back into my bulging, beefy shoulders.

Sproot! Sproot!

The bones broadened, following the contours of my huge head, shot out, and flipped up into three-foot horns on each sharp, lethal side.

My skin darkened and thickened into a tough, coarse-haired hide.

My body was bloating, stretching and expanding, bulking out further and further, piling on pound after pound of sheer muscle.

My fingers melded together and were sucked back into my hands. Tough hooves banded around the edges like metal plates.

"I'm telling you, don't open that! I'm hauling African Cape buffalo here, mister, and I don't think you want to —"

"*Never* attempt to think for me." A cold, sinister voice. A voice I had heard before. A voice I would never forget.

Visser Three.

My morphing had stopped when I'd lost concentration.

I refocused. Fast.

Schloop! Schloop!

My ears elongated. Sort of stretched out, drooped, and grew fringed hair.

The latch on the double doors clunked open.

"I'm telling you guys, don't do this!"

"Shut up and get out of my way!" Visser Three roared.

Sproot!

A tail shot out of my hind end as the double doors swung wide.

"See, I told you —" The driver stopped, his

eyes wide with horror. "The restraints broke!" He backed away. "Run!"

"Don't be a fool," Visser Three snapped. "I —"

The Cape buffalo gave an explosive snort through its wide, quivering nostrils.

And immediately, without warning, my own buffalo instinct kicked in.

CHAPTER 5

Fury.

No fear.

Fight to defend. Fight the threat.

Protect the herd.

I tossed my head, blew a harsh whoosh of air from my nostril, and surged forward, heart pounding, fueled by rage and adrenaline.

"Run!" the driver shrieked, taking off.

The pitch of his screams hurt my ears and my hair-trigger temper exploded. Hooves clattering, I burst out of the truck like a tornado, slashing and hooking, slamming into cars and trampling Controllers beneath my powerful legs.

More screams. Shouts.

Human-Controllers fleeing in all directions.

Dashing between the crooked, haphazardly parked cars. Hiding behind them. Hiding in them.

I saw them through a gray haze of fury, smelled their terror and followed it. No puny car could block my path.

Howls of pain.

I wheeled, broadsiding a human-Controller, sent him spinning.

Attack the threat! Destroy the threat!

Normally I was a calm, peaceful, grazing animal.

Until I was threatened. Provoked.

And then, nothing could stop me.

"Call the cops!" someone yelled. "Call back to The Gardens and get a tranquilizer gun out here!"

"Where's 'here'?!" another voice shouted.

"The woods along the highway! Outside the back gate! Hurry!" the guy hollered, crouching on top of his car.

<Cassie?>

The word echoed faintly in my enraged brain.

I ignored it.

I was a pile driver, wrecking anything and everything in my path.

<Cassie, I'm guessing that's you. Look, you have to get control,> Tobias said frantically. <They're calling your mom! She's bringing a tranquilizer gun! Cassie, where's the morphing cube?>

25

Huh? Who cares about some cube? Wait. Hang on. The box. Oh, yeah.

I fought the powerful animal's fury for a moment. Struggled to subdue its instincts and pull my human self back into consciousness.

"Two! There's two! Look out!"

I turned and saw the Cape buffalo I'd acquired pounding out of the truck, charging people with its horns and growing more agitated when it missed them.

Then it whirled and stampeded straight for Chapman. The assistant principal of our school. Member of The Sharing. And a high-ranking Controller.

THUD!

Chapman flew through the air and hit the ground with the same dull "whump" a watermelon makes when you drop it.

<Come on, Cassie!> Tobias yelled. <Get the cube and get moving!>

I ran back toward the truck. Stopped. Powered up my short, stocky legs and body-slammed Visser Three's limo with everything I had.

CRRRRUUUNNNCCCHHH!

The car alarm went off.

EEEUUUUU! EEEEUUUU! EEEEEUUUU!

The real Cape buffalo was going berserk. Smashing cars. Goring headlights. Bellowing and snorting and roaring with rage.

Panting, I leaped back into the truck, grabbed the blue box in my mouth, and barreled back out onto the highway.

I saw it all in one second.

Chapman, down and out on the pavement.

Cars wrecked and crumpled, Controllers sitting on top of them, clutching the roofs and looking petrified.

Visser Three, surrounded by a protective wall of frightened Controllers, screaming out enraged orders.

The original Cape buffalo, thundering across a field and into the woods.

I ran. The buffalo's herd instinct surged and I ran.

CHAPTER 6

I crashed through the underbrush, trampling saplings and ripping through sticker bushes without a second thought.

The scent of the real Cape buffalo was thick in my nostrils. I followed it deeper and deeper into the woods until the screams and shouts of the Controllers back at the roadblock were completely lost.

The buffalo's hearing — my hearing now — absorbed and gauged every sound, checking for any potential threat to my herd.

My depth perception wasn't so great, but I had a three-hundred-and-sixty-degree, wide-angle range of vision, which was going to make it pretty tough for anyone to sneak up on me.

This was a good thing.

I couldn't run very fast — nowhere near the speed of my wolf morph — but what the buffalo lacked in miles per hour, it definitely made up for in sheer bulk and muscle. Nobody, and I mean *nobody* — except maybe a lion — would take me on, and I could still outrun a lion if I had to.

And then there was man. The most infuriating scent, the most unnatural threat.

But the air was clean of man-scent.

The buffalo's brain, so powerful in its fury, began to shift its concentration in the quiet woods. Sort of downgraded from an all-out, fight-to-the-death attack mode to a standby alert that noted all sights, scents, and sounds, then dismissed them as nonthreatening.

It was a relief. It allowed me to get a firmer grip on the buffalo's natural instincts.

<Okay, Cassie, I told Jake you got away and you're all clear to demorph,> Tobias said, wheeling high in the sky above me. <The helicopters are still back over The Gardens trying to track down the others. Chapman got up but they loaded him into an ambulance. The Controllers are going nuts because they had to call in a whole fleet of tow trucks and Visser Three's limo's a total disaster.>

<Yeah, I guess my buffalo buddy and I got a little carried away,> I said, kind of embarrassed.

I found a dense bramble thicket where I could demorph, then, thinking twice, moved on until I was in a small clearing surrounded by a few trees. The thorns and stickers might not have hurt the buffalo's tough hide but they would've ripped my skin to shreds.

<Tobias, has anyone come up with a plan for destroying the Helmacron ship's sensors yet?>

<No, but we're going to have to figure out something fast. Definitely before those helicopters decide to change their focus and come after the box again.> Tobias swooped down and landed on a nearby branch.

I opened my mouth and dropped the slippery, spit-covered box on the ground. Then focused on my own DNA and felt the changes begin.

Even though everyone says I have a talent for morphing — and I have to admit I usually can sort of control the process — it still doesn't follow any real, precise pattern. So I wasn't surprised when the first thing to go this time was my tail. It drooped slowly and then started to melt like hot wax, then —

SCHLOOP!

Was sucked right back up into my body.

Bones began to grind and crunch, reshaping themselves.

My eyes crawled closer together. My ears shriveled and shrank.

SPROOT! SPROOT!

Ten human toes shot out of the crumbling hooves. My bones adjusted and reformed into ankles, then knees, then hips. My massive horns crumpled, deflated, and rolled back up toward the cleft at the center of my head.

<Yuck,> Tobias said, ruffling his feathers and looking the other way. <No offense, Cassie, but that is really gross. I'm glad I haven't eaten anything in a while.>

I began to say, "I know," but it came out as, "waaaw waaw."

"I know," I repeated, once my jaw finished shrinking. I flexed my fingers, bent down, and picked up the box. "And I know something else, too. We might want to steer clear of the real buffalo if we can. I, uh, don't think it trusts humans very much."

<No problem,> Tobias said. <The last time I saw it was way ahead of you and still running.>

"Good," I said, exhaling. "The Gardens'll send out a search party and probably a helicopter . . ."

Oh, that was a nice picture. And just what we didn't need. My mother buzzing around the sky, searching for a lost Cape buffalo, while we dodged Yeerks in helicopters who were trying to kill us.

Tobias cocked his head. Listening. <Uh-oh.>

"What?"

<Tell you in a minute,> he said. I watched him lift off, make a quick circle. <Helicopter, Cassie. The Yeerks are expanding their search. We'd better get going.>

"Are you sure it's the Yeerk helicopter, or is it the black one with a big 'The Gardens' logo on the side?" I asked.

<Yeerks,> he said tersely.

I took off at a trot, clutching the morphing cube and trying to keep to the soft carpet of pine needles since I was barefoot.

Tobias glided along only a few feet above my head. Every couple of minutes he'd flap hard for altitude, land in a treetop and check out the helicopter's progress.

<It's getting closer but it hasn't pinpointed us yet,> he said, swooping back down and landing on a tree branch a few yards ahead of me. <I —> His head jerked and he fell silent.

"What?" I said, huffing a little as I jogged toward him. "What, Tobias?"

And then I broke into the clearing and I saw for myself.

The Cape buffalo stood there, quivering. Twisting. Its eyes bulging with panic. Its mouth gaping in a silent scream. The scene was pretty bizarre all by itself. But in our world things always had to be slightly more than weird.

See, the Cape buffalo stood there, but instead of a Cape buffalo head and face was our assistant principal's.

Chapman.

CHAPTER 7

A freak of nature.

So help me, that's the first thought that swept into my mind, as I watched the buffalo stumble and squirm.

It sprouted a human leg covered with coarse, black animal hair.

Fringed, shaggy ears whipped out of Chapman's head, then shrunk into dachshund-sized ears.

<What the . . .> Tobias finally blurted, sounding a little nauseated.

"It's morphing," I whispered. I covered my mouth with my free hand and fell back a step. It was really terrible.

Chapman's skull split in the center and a pair of horns flowed from the crack like waves.

<How could it be morphing?> Tobias said, turning away and staring at me instead of the buffalo.

"It must have touched the blue box," I said helplessly, thinking back. I had laid the box down in the truck while I morphed . . .

"Oh, God. It saw me morph. In the truck. And then somehow, while I was out rampaging around the highway, it must have ripped free of its remaining restraints, brushed past the box, and then . . . It had plowed straight into Chapman and without even knowing it, had acquired his DNA."

I fell silent, not even realizing that I'd been speaking aloud.

<How could this happen?> Tobias asked, keeping his fierce, hawk's gaze fixed firmly on me. Like if he didn't see the buffalo, it wouldn't exist. <Cassie, we can't have an animal roaming around out here morphing Chapman! And what if it touches something else? What if it goes around acquiring, I don't know, *everything,* because it doesn't know any better!>

"It could, because it doesn't even know what's happening to itself," I said quietly, watching as the morph to Chapman finally became complete. "Look."

<I really don't want to,> he said, but did anyway.

The buffalo — Chapman — was down on all

35

fours, and though the human form was apparent it was covered in coarse hair — thankfully. Suddenly, it began tossing its head and making hooking movements even though it no longer had its horns. It snorted, then sniffed the air with its now-pitiful human nose. Slowly, watchfully, it lowered its head and bit off a mouthful of weeds.

"It's grazing," I said, feeling nauseous.

The buffa-human stiffened. It looked around, then spotted me. Issued a challenging snort and then a weak, warbling, "WAAAA!"

"I can't watch this anymore," I said, as the buffa-human — or Chapman or whatever it was — crawled and lurched toward me on its hands and knees. It was trying to charge, to hook me with its nonexistent horns, to kill me. To protect and defend.

I stepped aside as it lumbered past, its human head swinging and its tongue lolling out. Not even realizing it had missed me.

<This isn't *too* weird,> Tobias said, as the buffa-human stopped. Turned.

And slowly, creakily, straightened up onto its knees.

Wrong. It was all wrong! This terrible, twisted creature made my skin crawl. An adult — an assistant principal — was not supposed to huff and grunt and drool. Was not allowed to crawl and snort and pant. It betrayed everything I knew to be true about — about —

"It has a human brain, Tobias, but it doesn't have a clue as to what to do with it," I said, unable to stop staring at it, the way some people stare as they drive by car wrecks. It was grisly, it was gruesome, but I couldn't stop watching as the creature rose, wobbling and unsure, onto two legs. "Look, it's learning. It's watching me and learning!" The sight was both disturbing and exciting.

<Yeah, well, that's great except that we've got to get out of here,> Tobias said, flapping to the top of the tree for another helicopter check. <Oh, yeah. There's a whole group of people fanned out across the edge of the field and they're making their way over here.>

"We can't just leave it here," I said, watching as the buffa-human took a first shaky step toward me.

<Well, we can't take it with us!> Tobias said.

No we couldn't, not like this. But if I could get it to demorph back into its buffalo shape, then it would stop putting off so much morphing energy.

<Come on, Cassie, the Yeerks know at least one of those buffalo is giving off morphing energy —>

"Wait, Tobias. I'm going to morph back into

the buffalo to see if I can get it — him — to do it, too," I said. I focused on the powerful DNA swimming in my blood.

The buffa-human watched me, unblinkingly, as I fell forward onto four short, muscular buffalo legs.

My jaw ground and shifted into a long, hinged bovine one. My eyes slithered apart and my nose broadened. My nostrils stretched wide. Muscle upon muscle bulked up my body until I was huge and majestic and magnificent, with a tough hide and a hair-trigger temper.

But this time I was prepared for the buffalo's aggressive defenses, and I controlled them.

And then the other buffalo began to demorph.

Chapman's pale, human skin darkened and sprouted coarse hair. The flesh covering his bones shivered, rippled, and bent, forming into four bovine legs. His gaze remained locked onto mine as he fell forward, as his neck bulged —

And then the morph stopped.

<Come on,> I urged in thought-speak. I pushed aside the rising dominance I felt and moved slowly forward. Went nose-to-nose with the buffa-human in a sociable greeting. <Come on!>

The creature with Chapman's face stumbled backward, its legs thinning back to human's, fingers and toes bursting from its fading hooves.

<I don't get it. Why didn't it work? Two hours in morph and we'll have a really disturbing *nothlit* on our hands,> Tobias called from the treetop. <Cassie! We have to leave him here. The Gardens search team'll find him sooner or later!>

<What, as half-Chapman, half-buffalo? That's insane! We *can't* leave him! He doesn't even understand what's happening to him!> I cried.

I was frustrated because what Tobias said was absolutely true. We *did* need to go, but how could I have created such a mutation, even by mistake, and then abandon it — him?

I felt a little like a twenty-first-century Dr. Frankenstein and it was not a good feeling.

<Cassie, if we wait any longer . . .> Tobias warned.

<All right!> I shouted, then was immediately ashamed. <Sorry, Tobias.> I demorphed, avoiding the puzzled buffa-human's gaze, then, even though I was exhausted, immediately began to morph to wolf.

Thick shaggy fur sprouted all over my body. My spine stretched and crackled. The palms of my hands puffed and hardened into thick, protective pads.

My skull shattered and ground into a canine skull. My snout shot out and my teeth grew into long, lethal fangs.

The buffa-human snorted and tossed his human head. His torso was all bulky buffalo, his head and legs pathetically human. He was grotesque.

He lumbered toward me but I was a wolf now, and I moved with easy grace and lightning quickness.

<Okay, Tobias,> I called, picking up the morphing cube with my mouth. <I'm outta here. You fly back and get the others. I'll meet you guys up ahead.>

<Alone,> Tobias said, glancing pointedly at the odd mix of buffalo and human, and then launching himself into the air.

I looked at the creature, who was standing there, watching me.

<Alone,> I whispered, turning away in shame.

Because one way or another, his life as a normal African Cape buffalo was completely over.

As a creature morphing, he would draw the Helmacron sensors. And if he exceeded the two-hour limit in morph, he'd become some kind of hideous *nothlit.* Forever a mutant. Even if The Gardens found him, they wouldn't know what to do with him.

And I knew I was leaving him to die.

CHAPTER 8

I ran hard for a long time. Trying to put that last picture of the buffa-human out of my mind. Trying to forget how he'd started to follow me and how his plaintive, bewildered grunting still echoed through my head.

Leaving him was wrong. But I had done it anyway.

I had abandoned an animal with human DNA in its bloodstream.

Thwok thwok thwok!

I glanced up. Spotted a lone helicopter with no logo on the side.

The ominous drone was growing closer.

I paused, trying to figure out what to do.

In morph I was sending a stronger signal and

the helicopter could keep an easy lock on me. If I quickly demorphed back to human — besides that one fast burst of energy — I'd be giving off no signal except for the energy from the cube, and maybe I could lose them again.

Hunkering down on my haunches, I crept into the hollow beneath a clump of bushes and demorphed in record time.

Thwok! Thwok! Thwok!

The trees stirred and the darkening sky vibrated with the dull, thundering rumble of the sharp, swishing blades.

Time to run.

I crawled out and took off, zigzagging through the forest. I was cold, clumsy, slow. Twilight had fallen and I couldn't see well in the growing darkness. My feet were battered and bruised.

But what I was losing in miles I was making up for in confusion. The Yeerks in the helicopter kept losing the cube's signal and wheeling off in other directions, circling wider and wider until they were far enough away for me to pause, rest, and take off again.

So this is how the hunters do it, I thought, trying to catch my breath as I staggered through the shadows. *They don't even have to get dirty or tired. They can just sit in helicopters, probably drinking coffee, and chase their prey until it collapses.*

The helicopter's ominous THWOK! THWOK! THWOK! had returned and it was directly above me now, running me ragged, beating me down until I had no strength left and my pounding heart seemed ready to explode. I felt the same sick, terrified desperation of the hunted, powerless to shake the ominous, stalking specter of death.

I veered right in an effort to throw them off.

Dragged myself under a rock ledge to re-morph.

I *had* to break the lock the Helmacron sensors had on me. Weaken the signal.

THWOK! THWOK! THWOK!

If I didn't, the Yeerks would seize the blue box.

They'd hold me down as a Yeerk slug slithered into my ear and wove through my brain. I'd become a Controller, and then the Yeerks would know everything. That the "Andalite bandits" were really a bunch of human kids. They'd know where we lived, went to school, even what we ate. They'd know our families and take them, too.

They might even kill us. But they wouldn't kill Ax. Ax would be given to a Yeerk up-and-coming in the ranks. We all knew that another Andalite body, even one that was really just a kid's, was a coup.

They would find out about the Chee and annihilate them, extinguishing a race that had been around for millions of years. They would find out about the hidden colony of free Hork-Bajir and about the small but growing Yeerk resistance.

If I didn't find a way to break this sensor lock we were all dead.

I closed my eyes. Gathered up my shredded concentration.

Thwok! Thwok! Thwok!

I sat up and opened my eyes. Listened.

No, I hadn't imagined it. The treetops had stopped shaking and the leaves had stopped swirling around me.

The helicopter had moved off.

Exhausted, trembling, I grabbed the blue box and crawled out from under the bushes. Lay back on the carpet of pine needles and listened to the helicopter's faint thrumming. Watched as an assortment of owls and other birds of prey landed around me and began to demorph.

"Cassie?" Jake said, when he'd finished demorphing. "Are you all right?"

No, I definitely wasn't all right. I knew I was going to have to get up somehow, find the energy to morph again, and keep on running.

"I'm fine," I lied. Being an Animorph had made lying a necessary evil. For all of us.

"Good, because I've got some pretty decent

news," Jake said, smiling. "Erek rigged up a device that simulates morphing energy and planted it back at the far edge of the woods. Once the Yeerks find it they'll know it's a fake, but at least it'll buy us some time to figure out what to do."

So. I hadn't saved us by demorphing that last time. The Yeerks had been lured away by a stronger signal in another direction. Figures.

"The Chee are taking our places at home, so we're covered for the night," Rachel added, glancing around. "I should've stayed in owl morph. How are we supposed to find a place to hide while we make a plan if we can't even see where we're going?"

"We should go wolf," I answered. "That way we can move quickly and I can carry the morphing cube. I'm pretty sure there's a cave a few miles from here. The one I found when I was lost with Karen." The thought of Karen gave me a good feeling. She was a little girl who'd been infested by a Yeerk. But now she was free and the Yeerk had become part of the Yeerk peace movement. The thought also helped me remember that a few good things have happened to us since all this started. I guess that stands for something.

The next voice I heard was Tobias's. <I filled them in on the buffalo, Cassie. They thought of something we didn't. Actually, Ax thought of it.>

45

I turned to look at Ax.

He stared back with two of his four eyes. His stalk eyes were in constant movement, scanning the dark woods. His scorpion tail was curved high and ready to strike.

"And?" I said wearily.

<Tobias told us that this mutant learned to stand by observing you,> Ax continued. <And if he learns to speak, he will, most likely, be able to identify you.>

"Forget learning to speak," I interrupted, realizing what I hadn't realized before. "He's seen me morph! If the Yeerks infest him and are able to tap into his memories . . ."

<Human *or* buffalo,> Tobias added quietly. <It's seen you morph while it was in both forms.>

CHAPTER 9

Wolves can move. Quickly. Quietly. And for a very long time. The five of us blew through the woods until we finally found the cave. Tobias stayed overhead. Our own personal eye in the sky.

The helicopter was a constant presence, beating through the night sky like a distant pulse, rising and falling, keeping us on edge and very, very aware of every movement. And every shadow.

The cave itself was little protection from the Yeerk shock troops. But the feeling that comes from being walled-in on three sides was false security enough for us to be able to rest for a little while.

The sun set as we huddled in the gray light.

Well, I huddled. Rachel paced. Tobias perched on a low-hanging branch just outside the cave's entrance where Ax was keeping watch. Jake was sitting close by.

"Have I mentioned to all of you how much I hate this?" Marco grumbled, his voice eerily disembodied in the dim light. "I mean, it just doesn't stop."

"Neither does your mouth," Rachel retorted automatically, "C'mon, Jake, we need a better plan than just playing Keep Away."

"I know," Jake said, his fingers creeping over mine. "Any suggestions?"

"Well, I guess we have to find a way to disable the Helmacron sensors or destroy the ship, because no matter where we hide the cube, the sensors will find it," I said.

Marco snorted. "Do you think? You mean all we have to do is find a way to dodge the sensors and get up to the helicopter? All the while, we fight off the Yeerks' goon squad, find a puny, ultra-microscopic device, and smash it before we're either killed or captured. No problem-o."

<And don't forget about the buffa-human,> Tobias said.

"That one's easy," Rachel said dismissively. "We just have to get rid of it."

"But he's already acquired human DNA," I protested.

"So what? You're saying if we kill it, it's murder?" Rachel asked. "Come *on,* Cassie, it's not a human any more than I'm a bear or you're a wolf —"

"Or I'm a big monkey," Marco added.

Silence.

"Okay, so maybe Cassie does have a point," Jake said, obviously trying not to laugh.

"Nice," Marco smirked. "Very nice, *Prince* Jake."

Ax swiveled an eyestalk in Jake's direction. <Prince Jake, Marco and Rachel do make a valid point. I, too, have acquired human DNA. Does this make me a human rather than an Andalite?>

Silence.

"I hate these kinds of questions." Rachel. "There are never any concrete answers! I say we do whatever we have to do to protect ourselves and if that includes killing a buffalo, well, too bad. We know firsthand that cows die every day to make hamburgers —"

"Not in the school cafeteria," Marco said. "I'm pretty sure that's roadkill."

"Marco, let me ask you a question."

"Shoot."

"Is there any part of 'shut up' that you *don't* understand? 'Cause I'd be happy to explain it to you."

"C'mon, guys," Jake said impatiently. "We don't have a lot of time here."

He was right. We didn't know where the buffalo was or if the Yeerks had already captured it . . .

I shuddered. Forced myself not to mention the horrible possibility out loud.

The helicopter's engine still pulsed through the night like a dull heartbeat. A little louder. A little closer.

Jake sighed. "Yeah, well, we don't know anything for sure right now, except that we have to destroy those sensors if we plan on seeing our next birthdays."

<Okay, so how can we get inside the helicopter?> Tobias asked, sounding strained.

Jake looked toward the cave entrance and then back to us. "Why go inside it?"

"How are we supposed to destroy the sensory devices if we don't get inside the helicopter that's carrying them?" Rachel asked.

"Maybe we should take down the whole helicopter," Jake said. "Don't even risk going inside. We already know we don't exactly want to get up close and personal with Taxxons or Hork-Bajir if we can avoid it."

"I agree," I said. Hork-Bajir were lethal enough with their razor-bladed bodies, but the Taxxons — gigantic, cannibalistic centipedes with incredibly sharp teeth — were just disgusting. The stuff nightmares are made of.

"So, how do we take down a helicopter?" Rachel said. "We've totally lost the element of surprise."

"No surprise," Jake said. "We give the Yeerks what they want. We let them get a good look at the morphing cube —"

<Uh, Jake?> Tobias said. <Isn't that a little risky? I mean, you know that Visser Three *wants* this cube. What if once he's absolutely sure we've got it with us, he sends a whole Hork-Bajir army to get it? We're good, but we're not that good.>

"Exactly, and here's where the fake-out comes in," Jake said. "Once the Yeerks pinpoint the source of the morphing energy, 'cause we let them 'catch us,' they're going to be on the lookout for a trap, right?"

"Ooookay," Marco said.

"So we give them one, only not from the direction they expect."

<Prince Jake, exactly what is the meaning of "fake-out"? I am not sure I understand,> Ax asked.

"You're not the only one," Rachel muttered.

"Okay, look," Jake said, sighing. "The guys in the helicopter are hunting the source of the morphing energy. We're it. We let the cube be

51

spotted and then take off. While they're trying to run us to ground, one of us hangs back and ambushes them."

"Brilliant!" Marco stood up and applauded. "One of us against a bunch of Controllers in a helicopter. Which, I'm guessing, just guessing, is equipped with a bunch of weapons. What's the plan, morph a bird and peck the copter to death? Splatter poop all over the windshield and hope it crashes?"

"We could try to lure it down to the ground," Rachel offered. "And then attack it and destroy the Helmacron ship."

Marco shook his head. "Like they won't be expecting that."

"Do you have a better idea?" Rachel snapped.

"I kinda like the peck-'n'-poop thing, myself," he said brightly.

"You know, birds get sucked into airplane engines and cause crashes all the time," I said quietly, tightening my grip on Jake's hand.

<Ugh,> Tobias said uneasily. <Not a good way to go.>

"So, you're saying we do a suicide run?" Rachel said.

"Well —" Jake began.

"No," Marco interrupted. "Not a suicide run, a cartoon run! Oh, man, I am so good! Listen, what does Wile E. Coyote do when he wants to squash the Road Runner?"

"He straps one of those Acme rockets to his back," Rachel said. "Dive-bombs him or something."

Marco slapped his forehead and groaned. "Noooo! Come on, am I the only one educated in cartoon combat?" We all stared at Marco. "Oh, for . . . He drops an anvil on him! Don't you get it? We need to drop an anvil on the helicopter!"

"Ahhh," Jake said slowly. "Okay, yeah. It's perfect. We can't do it over the woods, though. The last thing we need is to cause a fire or something."

Everything was falling into place. "We lure the helicopter out over the ocean. And then we drop the anvil," I said calmly.

Jake smiled. "The sooner we get this done, the better. This is going to take split second timing to pull off."

<Jake?> Tobias said urgently. <Someone's coming. Taxxons.>

"Morph," Jake ordered. "Now!"

CHAPTER 10

I morphed.

I concentrated on the DNA and within a heartbeat, powerful horns popped through my scalp and were flowing and curving down the sides of my head and ending in sharp, deadly spears.

My internal organs slithered and gurgled, swimming and settling into my expanding bulk.

SPROOT!

My tail shot out.

My teeth grew, crowding my jaw and flattening into grinding molars. Coarse black hair sprouted and spread across my muscular tank body.

And when the African Cape buffalo's mind

rose, I was ready. Got a lock on the aggressive, hair-trigger temper.

<The Taxxon trackers have spotted the cave, Prince Jake,> Ax said tensely. <I would not advise getting trapped in here.>

He was right. I glanced over at Jake, who'd morphed a sleek, deadly tiger.

At Rachel, a massive, towering grizzly bear.

Marco, a gorilla with enormous hands and the strength to tear a human apart limb from limb.

At Ax and Tobias who'd chosen their own forms. An Andalite whose razor-tipped tail was as lethal as lightning and twice as fast. And a red-tailed hawk with talons created to puncture, rip, and tear.

<I'll go first.> Jake padded silently to the edge of the cave.

I followed him, the blue box wedged tightly in my mouth.

Clop clop clop!

<C'mon, Cassie, let's get movin', ole girl,> Marco joked, slapping me on the rump.

The buffalo temper flared and I twisted, tossing my horns at him.

<Whoa! Watch it, will you? You almost gutted me!> he said, leaping back just in time.

<Sorry about that,> I muttered.

I followed the others cautiously out of the cave, relying more on my sense of smell and hearing than on my eyesight. I was listening for even the slightest whisper of sound.

<We've got trouble,> Jake said.

<No problem.> Rachel threw back her head and let out an enraged roar.

"GGGGRRRRRRROOOAARRR!"

The night erupted.

The buffalo's overwhelming defense instincts kicked in and suddenly I was barreling through the weeds, tossing my horns, and impaling a Taxxon where it stood.

"SSSKKKRRREEE!" It fell, writhing and twisting, foul-smelling blood pumping from its wounds.

Immediately, two other Taxxons converged and tore it to shreds.

I began to bellow, enraged by the scent of aggression, by the invasion and threat to my herd.

WHAM!

I charged, slamming one of the feeding Taxxons into a tree. It burst, spewing guts everywhere. Frenzied, I trampled the second Taxxon, piercing its fat, squishy body with my hooves.

It slashed at me, spasming in its death throes, but I barely felt its needle teeth. My heart was thundering and adrenaline powered my massive body.

Nothing hurt. And nothing could stop me.

"SSSRRREEE WAAAARRI!"

I whirled and saw Jake rake open a Taxxon.

"RRRROOOOOWWWRRR!"

Rachel, slashing and biting at a pair of Hork-Bajir, her chest matted with blood.

Fury rose and I stampeded a Hork-Bajir.

WHUMPF!

Its fiercely bladed arm split my shoulder.

I gored it, trampled it. Backed off.

It didn't move.

FWAP! FWAP!

Ax's tail blade was slicing and dicing, severing Hork-Bajir arms, hands, landing lethal blows, but there were too many and he was being driven back toward the cave.

A furious, gray haze misted my vision and I barreled through the Hork-Bajir, a tank, a steamroller, hooking them, goring them, scattering them like bowling pins.

More Hork-Bajir converged, wrist and arm blades slashing.

"TSSSSEEEER!" Tobias screeched, raking his talons across a Hork-Bajir's eyes.

It screamed.

Everyone was screaming.

Marco bellowed. Bringing down his huge fist onto a Taxxon. But his scalp was split, and one of his ears was missing.

<There're too many!> he yelled.

"GGRRROOOWWWWWR!" Rachel roared, as

a Hork-Bajir blade carved a deep swath through her shoulder.

Jake leaped, grabbing a Taxxon and taking it down, ripping at it with his back claws. Leaped away and took down another one. <Keep fighting! If we retreat now, we're dead!>

I slammed into another Hork-Bajir. And another. Stomped them. Gored them.

Their blades sank deep into my hide, slicing me open, nicking my bones and making me scream in pain, making me charge in fury, making me fight to the death.

<I'm losing it, Jake!> Marco yelled, clutching his head and reeling away from a downed Taxxon.

<Prince Jake, we have to stop,> Ax said grimly, lopping the head off a slavering, chittering Taxxon. <We are severely outnumbered —>

That's when I heard the familiar bellowing. The enraged bellow was fresh and furious.

<It's the buffalo, Cassie!> Tobias shouted. <The Yeerks didn't get it!>

I sucked in lungfuls of air and let out a resounding, answering snort.

The buffalo went berserk. It was a whirlwind of destruction. Trampled, pierced, gored, and gouged huge, gaping holes in the Taxxons. Battered the Hork-Bajir.

We all went a little crazy after that, on some

kind of sick, bloody rampage spurred on by the African Cape buffalo who annihilated the Hork-Bajir ranks with sheer savagery. And finally, sent them howling, bent and broken, into the forest.

And then it was over.

CHAPTER 11

We were all pretty messed up. So with Ax and Tobias keeping a lookout and the buffalo following doggedly at our heels, we demorphed.

The buffalo watched us, then began its own morph.

Once again, unnervingly, the head developed first.

"Of all the people around, it just had to acquire Chapman?" Marco joked lamely, turning away. "That is so not cool."

<I don't think there was a lot of choice involved there,> Tobias said.

"It's becoming human," I said quietly, watching as the buffalo's skin faded and lightened, as the coarse hairs were sucked back into its body.

<It doesn't know what it's doing, Cassie,> Tobias said.

CCRRACK!

The buffalo's legs reversed, stretched, and hinged into human knees.

"There's something really gross about this," Rachel said, shaking her head. "It's so, I don't know, unnatural."

"So are we," I said, watching as the buffa-human wobbled up onto two feet.

Jake shot me a concerned look.

"That's different," Marco said. "We morph consciously. This buffalo's just mimicking what it sees. It doesn't know what the heck is going on."

"But what if it could learn?" I said. "What if now that it has a human brain, he learns to use it? What if it learns how to reason, or —"

"Nuh," the buffa-human grunted. "Guhhr-nuh." It looked up at me and blinked.

"It's learning to talk," I said, feeling a mixture of hope and nausea.

"No way," Marco shot back. "That was just some kind of weird, random firing of neurons in the speech part of its brain."

"You're wrong," I said, stepping slowly toward the buffa-human, who went very still. "Hi. I know you can't understand me yet —"

"Nuh," it grunted, tossing its head. "Uhh-hhnnn."

"Hi," I repeated.

"Heeeeehhhhh," it said, looking puzzled.

"I wouldn't push too hard to teach it to talk, Cassie," Jake warned. "If it becomes too human, it's gonna be a problem."

"Trust me, Jake, it's not gonna live that long," Rachel snapped. "I'm not being handed to the Yeerks by some lame Chapman mutation."

Thwok thwok thwok!

<Helicopter,> Tobias said tensely.

"We'll have to morph," Jake said, running a hand through his hair. "We don't have a choice. Everyone use your wolf morphs."

Thwok thwok thwok!

I concentrated on the wolf DNA. Immediately, a ruff of thick, lush fur sprouted around my neck. My legs dwindled in size but didn't weaken. My chest and shoulders swelled, and my face began to bulge. My teeth grew into long, deadly fangs.

The buffa-human was morphing, too. Watching me as its defenseless, human body beefed up until it was a dark, massive rock. As the rolling, deadly horns sprouted from the center of its skull.

Mimicking.

THWOK! THWOK! THWOK!

The trees whipped wildly and dirt flew.

I scooped up the blue box in my mouth.

<Let's haul!> Jake ordered, streaking out of the clearing.

We dashed after him, slipping away into the darkness just as a blinding shaft of light pierced the clearing from above.

<Wait!> I shouted. <The buffalo!>

<We can't wait!> Rachel said, tearing past me.

<But we can't leave it!> I cried, pacing anxiously in the dense shadows.

<Come on, Cassie! It's not in morph. If it runs away, it won't draw the Helmacron sensors. We will, so let's go!> Jake said.

The real buffalo bellowed and snorted and barreled after me, bringing the searchlight with it.

I couldn't kill it and I couldn't let it reach me. If it did, the Yeerks would see the morphing cube in my mouth. And that just wasn't going to happen.

Whirling, I shot off after the others.

I could hear the buffalo crashing along behind me, snapping trees and crushing anything in its path.

The helicopter blades sliced through the air but I was already pulling ahead of the buffalo, dodging and racing through the woods.

TSSSEEEWW!

A pine tree behind me exploded.

TSSEEWW!

KA-BOOM!

A huge boulder blew apart, winging fragments like shrapnel.

<Bug fighters,> I heard Ax say grimly.

<No kidding,> Marco said.

"SSSSRRRREYYYAA SSSEEWWWITT!"

A pair of Taxxons burst through the bushes in front of Tobias.

"Grrr GrrOWWWRR!" I dropped the blue box and launched myself at the closest one. Felt its rows of tiny legs scrabbling through my fur. Sank my teeth into its disgusting body and twisted, yanking and tearing its flesh.

It screamed.

I bit it again, sinking my muzzle into its guts and ripping them out of its body.

I left it dead, and helped Tobias finish off the other one. Trotted back and picked up the blue box.

<Thanks,> Tobias said, running alongside me. <I didn't even see them coming.>

<Don't do that again, Cassie,> Jake called back sternly. <Don't leave that morphing cube anywhere. There could have been another Taxxon waiting to grab it! And then what?>

He was right, but his scolding tone still hurt.

<Sorry,> I mumbled.

<Rachel, drop back behind Cassie,> Jake instructed. <And if there are any more attacks —>

<I'll handle it,> Rachel promised, circling back around me.

I felt like a total idiot. Like I should have known better. Only I couldn't have stood there and let the Taxxons rip Tobias apart, could I? No.

<He's worried about you, Cassie,> Rachel said to me, in private thought-speak.

<He should trust me to do the right thing,> I said.

<He does, or he would've made somebody else carry the cube. That's why he put me back here. While you do the right thing, I do the necessary thing. Get it?>

<Well, when you put it that way,> I said, mollified.

SLASH! CCRRAAAAAAAACK!

Hork-Bajir exploded out of the woods around us.

And somewhere up ahead, I heard Jake howl in pain.

CHAPTER 12

It was total mayhem.

Screams. Shouts.

Grunts of pain.

Snarling.

Rachel shot past me, a lethal blur of fur and teeth. Launched herself at the closest Hork-Bajir and ripped its throat out.

That's when the buffalo came up from behind me and charged into the fray, slamming and trampling Hork-Bajir, mindless of its own open wounds.

TSEEEEW! TSSEEEW!

The clearing lit up with a blinding flash and another tree exploded.

I couldn't drop the blue box, so I couldn't fight. Couldn't help my friends. I was glad the buffalo had followed us, glad to see it take my place in battle, but I was afraid, too. If the Hork-Bajir-Controllers noticed I wasn't fighting, noticed my jaws weren't free to defend myself . . .

I hunkered down and belly-crawled under a thick bush.

THWOK! THWOK! THWOK!

The helicopter hovered directly above us. The downwash pounded us with dirt and pine needles and rubble. The spotlight flooded the clearing. There really was no place to hide.

It was a bloody, gruesome scene.

Severed Hork-Bajir arms and legs twitching in the dirt. Growing pools of blood. Taxxons feasting, drooling, like something out of a slasher movie — only this was real.

TSEEEWWW!

I bolted out from under the bush.

The spot near where I'd been hiding exploded in a shower of rocks and dirt.

<Run, Cassie!> Jake shouted. <Just go! Head for the beach! We're right behind you!>

Leave them and run? I paused in the shadows, torn.

THWOK! THWOK!

TSEEEW!

A pine tree shattered.

The spotlight shifted toward me. Searching for the morphing energy.

Searching for the blue box.

We took off, zigzagged, and somehow managed to lose the helicopter. The Bug fighters swooped and zipped through the sky, blasting anything and everything that moved, but at least they were still focused on the woods behind us.

<For now I guess they think we should be too beat-up to run,> Marco said, limping.

<Good,> Jake said, padding along beside me. <Let them keep thinking that.> He glanced at me. <You okay?>

<Yeah,> I said shortly, tightening my jaws around the blue box.

He must have noticed my tone, because he said in private thought-speak, <I'm sorry I yelled at you before. It kind of came out wrong.>

<That's okay,> I said, too weary to hold a grudge. <I understand. We can't lose the blue box, no matter what.>

<The forest is thinning and there is a road up ahead, Prince Jake,> Ax said, slowing. <Should we keep going?>

<Yeah, we're going to have to cross it to get to the beach,> Jake said.

<There's probably going to be a whole mess of them patrolling the road,> Tobias said quietly.

<Controllers,> Rachel sneered.

And probably even more Hork-Bajir, I thought.

We crept beneath huge clumps of sticker bushes lining the edge of the road.

<All right, I'm open for suggestions,> Marco said. <How do we get across without being seen?>

<Morph to flies,> Rachel said immediately.

<Flies can't carry the blue box,> Jake pointed out.

<Okay, so I'll morph elephant, kick some butt, and carry it across myself,> Rachel snapped back.

<Not a good idea,> Marco said. <We've been doing okay so far because the goon squad's been so spread out searching for us. Now they know we're in the area and they're gonna swarm us. We don't need to advertise exactly where we are. Yet.>

<Do you have a better idea?> Rachel said sweetly, which for Rachel usually means she'd like to punch you in the face.

We shrank back from the road as a patrol car cruised slowly past, shining its spotlight into the woods.

<Well, we'd better think of something because the longer we stay here, the better our chances of getting caught,> Jake said. <Especially if that buffalo catches up to us again.>

<But when it's not morphing, it's not giving off any morphing energy,> I said.

<No, but it's not exactly the quiet type, either, Cassie,> Marco said. <It just charges in like . . . well, like a big ole buffalo.>

<Don't worry,> I said, with a confidence I didn't really feel. <We left it way behind us.>

Marco looked at me. I turned away first.

<We could break down the cube and each carry a piece across the road,> Tobias suggested, getting us back on track.

<No, because we'd still have to use morphs big enough to be seen,> Jake said.

And then it came to me. Pure. Simple. Ridiculously simple.

<Throw it,> I said.

<What?> Jake said, startled.

<Rachel said it before. It's like playing Keep Away,> I said. <We morph into flies, cross the road and demorph. One of us stays behind, demorphs, and throws the box over the road when nobody's looking. The rest of us get it, the thrower morphs to fly, buzzes over, and we're gone! Simple.>

<That's a lot of morphing energy in one place,> Tobias said uneasily. <We're bound to draw the Helmacron sensors and the helicopter. And then come the ground forces.>

<But staying here will also allow the Hel-

macron sensors to determine our location,> Ax pointed out.

Thwok thwok thwok!

The helicopter.

<Okay, let's do it,> Jake said. <Sorry, Rachel. That's your line.>

<I'll let it slide this time,> she said. <But don't let it happen again.>

It was a simple plan and it should have been easy.

I should have known better.

CHAPTER 13

Demorph.

Remorph to flies. Marco to human since he'd decided to be the one to toss the cube.

Exhausting.

But necessary.

Huge, glittering, bulging compound eyes popping out of my sockets.

Legs sprouting from my chest, gauzy wings tearing through my back and unfurling.

Crunching, mushing, gurgling gut-shifting.

And the long, tubular proboscis stretching out of the middle of my fly face.

My wings beat two hundred times a second. I gave into the rush, zipped up, and landed on Marco's nose.

"Hey," he whispered, swiping at me. "Who's the wise guy?"

<Sorry,> I said, buzzing circles around his head.

<Okay, people,> Jake said. <Marco, I'll let you know when we get across and demorph. Then you throw the cube to us. We'll grab it, you morph to fly, and then we're out of here.>

"Aye-aye, Captain," Marco said quietly, hunkering down in the bushes.

<Spread out, guys,> Jake called, buzzing away. <Meet you on the other side!>

I shot off after him. Now, a fly can only cover about four miles an hour, but when you're only an eighth of an inch long, that's like major warp speed. I stifled the urge to dip and dive, and powered in a straight line across the road.

Patrol car headlights cut through the darkness.

I shot straight up about a millisecond before the lights swept past.

<Made it,> Jake called, zipping down into a thick stand of weeds.

<I think I'm right behind you,> I said, landing and immediately beginning my demorph.

<We all here?> Jake asked, when he'd finished demorphing and had remorphed back into a wolf.

<I think we are all here, Prince Jake,> Ax said, joining the rest of us.

Morphing is tiring and doing rapid morphing, like from a wolf to a human to a fly, then from a fly to a human to a wolf was more than we've ever had to do. But the wolf's sleek, powerful body was fresh and its senses keen, so the weariness wouldn't catch up with us until we were human again.

And when that happened, we were all going to sleep for a week.

Thwok thwok thwok!

<Okay, Marco, come on,> Jake called. <Wing it!>

Marco couldn't respond because he had demorphed.

<Two more patrol cars are coming,> Tobias said. <The helicopter must be picking up the morphing energy and radioing down to the cars.>

<We'll have to chance it anyway,> Jake said. <Throw it high, Marco, and then get over here!>

The blue box soared out of the bushes, up, up, up, arcing high over the center of the road.

Thwok! Thwok! Thwok!

The treetops began to sway in the downwash.

<The helicopter's coming!> Jake yelled. <Get over here, Marco! Hurry!>

A spotlight split the darkness, only feet from the soaring blue box.

I held my breath.

THWOK! THWOK! THWOK!

The helicopter hovered above the trees, kicking up whirling dirt devils and whipping the bushes into a frenzy.

The human-Controllers piled out of the cars, heads bent and eyes scrunched against the battering downwash.

<It's blowing the box right toward us!> I watched as the cube picked up speed and hurtled toward the ground. And then I bunched up my muscles, took a flying leap, and snatched it in my powerful jaws right before it crashed.

<Whoa! Nice catch!> Tobias said.

<Ow,> I mumbled, my tongue numb from the impact.

<I'm impressed,> Jake said. <Next time we play Frisbee, you're on my team.>

And then, everything fell apart.

The buffalo, nostrils twitching and head held high, stepped onto the road.

<Guess it can run faster than you thought, huh, Cassie?> Marco said dryly.

The buffalo gazed at the knot of human-Controllers gazing at it.

One of the cops made a quick motion and four or five Hork-Bajir stepped out of the woods and around the patrol cars.

The buffalo snorted and tossed its head.

I now knew what that motion meant. I had experienced it firsthand. Aggression. It was going to fight them. Defend the herd it'd been following all night.

<Prince Jake, this buffalo is quickly becoming a huge problem,> Ax said, his voice firm.

<Look at it,> Rachel said. <It's surrounded by Hork-Bajir? And it's going to fight them. I know a battle stance when I see one.> Grudging admiration tinged her voice. <It's going to fight them to the death.>

<Wrong,> Marco said. <The human-Controllers won't let it be killed. Not if Visser Three thinks its an Andalite.>

No winning this one. If the buffalo was killed in battle, we'd be safe. And our hands — my hands — wouldn't be stained with blood containing human DNA.

But I knew Marco was right. The Controller who caught a live "Andalite bandit" would probably be well rewarded. The Controller who killed it would be, well, probably dead himself.

We were going to have to destroy the buffalo. If we were closer to home, we might have been able to do it humanely, to euthanize it using my father's vet supplies. But I wasn't home. And now I didn't know when the chance would come, or what morph we would use to destroy such a powerful animal, but my stomach turned at the thought of pitting buffalo against buffalo.

<Cassie? I am sorry. But we cannot allow it to be captured,> Ax said quietly.

<Okay,> Jake said wearily. <Let's go rescue a buffalo.>

CHAPTER 14

The helicopter was coming straight toward us. The fighting stopped.

<Watch out!> I yelled. I shot beneath the skids and head-butted Jake with everything I had. Which was just enough to make him stumble out from beneath the rapidly descending helicopter.

<Oof!> he grunted. <Uh, thanks, Cassie. I think.>

<We're trapped,> Rachel said bitterly. <And all because of that stupid buffalo!>

I looked at the buffalo. Its flanks were heaving. It stood, head high, and stared at the figure emerging from the helicopter.

<Visser Three,> Ax announced coldly, in public thought-speak, as the leader of the Yeerk invasion leaped nimbly from the helicopter.

<Ah, Andalite scum,> Visser Three said almost graciously, glancing at us and chortling to himself. <How thoughtful of you to group together so that the Helmacron sensors would have no trouble locating you!> His gaze lingered on the buffalo standing nearby. <You have caused me much inconvenience this day. Now, let's make this simple, shall we? Where is the device?> He stepped up to the buffalo and jabbed a slender finger down into one of its gaping wounds. <Answer me, Andalite!>

The buffalo snorted and swung its head, its horn narrowly missing Visser Three. The visser moved away slowly, his main eyes half-mast. Almost as if he were drugged.

<Figures,> Marco muttered. <That big boy's got more lives than a cat.>

<Tell me where to find the morphing cube!> Visser Three roared. He'd obviously snapped out of his funk.

The Hork-Bajir cringed. So did the human-Controllers left standing. So did we.

I didn't look around. I stood with my head down, hiding the cube that was still tucked into my mouth.

<Or perhaps one of you has it with you now,> Visser Three said, in a suddenly low, silky voice. He turned away from the buffalo and glared at each of us. <Give it to me now or I will make you beg to die,> he said.

<Prince Jake, the buffalo is morphing,> Ax said urgently. <It acquired the visser!>

<Oh, man, this is too good!> Marco crowed.

While the real Visser Three was raging at the Hork-Bajir for not finding the cube, the buffalo was turning blue, growing eye stalks, and thin, almost graceful arms. Turning into an exact replica of the visser's stolen Andalite body.

Including a curved and lethal Andalite tail.

<It's probably now or never,> Jake said tensely. <When Visser Three turns around and sees that buffa-Andalite, we get out of here! Head straight for the beach!>

<What about the buffalo?> I asked. I watched as it experimentally flicked its tail, severing the arm of a Hork-Bajir in the process. <He doesn't know how to use that body!>

<It'll learn fast,> Jake said, as the Hork-Bajir cried out in pain.

Visser Three turned toward the sound.

<Now!> Jake shouted.

"Grrr GrrrOWWWRR!" I plowed through the terrified human-Controllers.

TSEEW! TSEEW!

<Get him!> Visser Three commanded, pointing imperiously at the buffalo in Andalite morph.

The buffalo pointed back, mimicking.

The Hork-Bajir-Controllers hesitated, torn between the two.

Visser Three's Andalite tail came up.

The buffa-Andalite's did, too.

FWAPP! Visser Three's tail lopped off one of the buffalo's Andalite arms.

The buffalo bellowed in open thought-speak and charged. Slapped and whipped its tail with little skill but with major fury. Drove Visser Three back.

The Hork-Bajir and human-Controllers milled in helpless confusion, not daring to attack the wrong visser.

<Now, now!> Jake yelled, charging into a knot of Hork-Bajir and plowing open a huge hole. He ran into the woods with us behind him, trampling anything that got in our way.

I wished I could call the buffalo after me. It had actually helped us fight and I didn't want to leave it behind to be killed. Or worse.

FWAPP! Visser Three's tail lashed out again.

One of the buffalo's eye stalks fell to the ground.

The buffalo's tail jerked forward, more of a pain reaction than anything, and the dull side of his tailblade whacked Visser Three on the side of his head.

He dropped like a stone.

The Hork-Bajir stood silent, uncertain.

The buffalo in the Andalite's body galloped through the Hork-Bajir and into the woods.

Following us.

CHAPTER 15

The beach was getting closer but we were wounded and tired.

I could hear the Hork-Bajir behind us, not right on our tails but gaining fast.

<Okay, guys.> Tobias had already demorphed and taken to the sky. <We're very close. We should hurry.>

Jake sighed. <Okay. This is it. It's almost over. Is everyone ready? Cassie?>

I shivered. So many things could go wrong.

<Visser Three knows for sure now that we've got the morphing cube with us,> Jake continued. <And when he wakes up he's going to be on us like white on rice.> He looked straight at me.

<We need someone to hang back here in the ravine and buy us some time.>

<I'll do it.> Rachel — of course.

<No, I will,> I said slowly. <I'm pretty sure the buffalo will stay and fight if I'm here in buffalo morph.>

And probably be killed. I felt like the worst of all traitors.

<Right,> Jake said. He nodded. <Okay, guys, we're out of here. Cassie?>

<Yeah?>

<See you at the water.> He took the cube in his mouth.

I hope so, I thought. But I didn't say it, not even in private thought-speak. Instead, I watched as they took off through the thinning forest.

The buffa-Andalite shifted.

I turned back to face it. It was wounded and bloody, its lone eye stalk drooping. Somehow, I had to get him to demorph back into his true buffalo self, where he was at his most lethal.

Where I could use him most effectively.

And I had to use my own buffalo morph so we could fight side by side with full power.

I focused on my human DNA. Demorphed as rapidly as I could, trying not to give the buffalo time to mimic me. I went from tired, wounded wolf to puny, human girl and then bulked right back up again, growing a fresh, thick hide and sharp, curving horns.

The buffalo began to darken and swell, mimicking my shape, demorphing back into his true form. It eyed me warily for a moment, then the tension eased. It had followed me as a Cape buffalo before and by doing so, had already established our hierarchy.

A twig snapped.

We both lifted our heads, noses twitching. Caught the scent of approaching danger. And knew to protect the herd.

I snorted.

It snorted.

We tossed our horns and I lumbered into the tall bushes, the buffalo following.

We would wait. And then we would ambush the Hork-Bajir. That's when I noticed the drop-off on the edge of the ravine. Not too far down but definitely far enough down to hurt.

They started to come at us quietly, cautiously, and within minutes.

We waited until they were almost equal with us and then . . .

I bulldozed out of the bushes, knocking down trees, goring and slashing as I allowed the buffalo's defense instincts to kick in and send me into a wild, raging fury.

And still more Hork-Bajir fought their way through the narrow ravine.

<Get out of my way!> Visser Three thundered at his troops.

My blood ran cold.

He was morphing. His stolen Andalite body bulging and melting, turning black and gooey. Oozing forward and tainting everything he touched. Making the nearby Hork-Bajir's skin sizzle and bubble like it was being dissolved with acid. Short, thick, dripping tentacles shot out of his body, and a huge, wet, red mouth with buzzsaw teeth chomped and smacked, drooling the same smoking, sizzling acid.

Time to go, I thought, as Visser Three pointed a tentacle at me.

A stream of acid flew through the air. It splattered the Hork-Bajir in front of me and sent it howling and writhing to the ground.

The holes in its skin bubbled and stank.

I wheeled.

Powered up my short, muscular legs.

And with a loud, snorting call to the buffalo, barreled to the edge of the drop-off and jumped.

CHAPTER 16

Terror. Sheer panic.

Falling was nothing like flying.

No control at all.

My buffalo instincts went insane.

I bellowed, legs scrabbling for something, anything, to hold on to. My heart slammed into my chest and panic froze my blood.

I crashed down through a thick, brittle layer of scrub bushes, falling . . .

The rocks shot up at me, hard and cruel and —

WHUMPF! CRRUNNCH!

I couldn't breathe. Couldn't move. Pain was everywhere, pounding and tearing at me.

WHUMPF! CRRAAACCCKKK!

The ground shook when the buffalo landed beside me.

I opened my eyes, dazed. And through a hazy mist of agony saw the buffalo raise its head and look at me. It bawled piteously and struggled to rise.

It couldn't. It had snapped a couple of legs; the bones jutted out through the torn, ragged skin. Blood pumped and stained the ground.

It was in agony, but it wasn't dying. Yet.

I was bleeding, too, from the branch that had speared into my stomach on the way down.

Infection's going to set in, I thought dimly. *Someone had better cleanse this wound really thoroughly or —*

No. No one was going to cleanse my wounds.

No one was going to save me.

The world got smaller, then expanded. I blinked, fighting the wooziness.

My blood was pumping out of my chest with every beat of my thundering heart. I would probably die before the buffalo did. If it did.

The buffalo bawled again. Its unbroken legs churned the dirt.

There was only one way to save us.

<Watch me,> I said to the buffalo.

Its head jerked and he focused its eyes upon me.

I began to demorph, slowly at first, then gaining speed.

My shattered bones ground and reformed.

"Come on," I urged, as the buffalo groaned and began to shift shape.

I crouched beneath the bushes beside it. Sickened by the transformation, yet unwilling to leave him there to die like this, or live on as a crippled bloody mess. Or be captured by the Yeerks.

A human head. Nose stretching, slimming. Eyes crawling from the sides to the front of the face. Teeth shrinking, ears popping out.

The buffa-human opened its eyes and looked at me.

"Come on," I said, when the morph was complete. I stood up.

The buffa-human — Chapman — got to his knees. Shakily, he rose onto two feet and swayed. Took a wobbly step toward me. Snorted.

I snorted back. "Come on."

We traveled slowly, keeping close to the drop-off base where the Hork-Bajir couldn't see us. We were safe for the moment. They weren't coming down the same way we did.

Visser Three knew it, too, and his enraged shouts echoed through the canyon.

The buffa-human stiffened at the sound. Tossed its head.

"Don't listen," I said, motioning it on after me. "Come on, we have to find the others."

But even as I said it, I was filled with a sick mixture of hope and dread. What was going to happen to this sad, messed-up creature when we did meet up with the rest of the "herd"?

We couldn't let it live and yet everything inside me rebelled at the thought of killing it. I could have let it die back there — Marco and Rachel would probably say I should have and Jake had expected me to — but I just couldn't. And I was at least partially responsible for its awful situation. To have walked away and left it when I knew a way to help it . . . Well, I just couldn't.

If it had to die, it had to die fast, without excess pain. Not lingering. Not inhumanely.

"Guuuuhhh," it said, stumbling along behind me on its tender, human feet. "Goowwww."

"You have to walk carefully," I said, pointing down at the smooth patch of rock I was standing on. "See?" I stepped on another smooth surface, avoiding a tangle of sticker bushes. "Like this."

The buffa-human frowned but stepped where I'd stepped. Its face cleared. "Guuhh."

"Yes, that's good," I said, my heart sinking right down to the bottom of my stomach. What was I doing? I shouldn't be talking to it — but I always talked to the wounded animals in my father's Wildlife Rehab, especially when I was changing their bandages or cleaning their cages. Calm words seemed to soothe them —

But this was different and I knew it.

"There she is! Cassie!"

The shout was faint.

I looked up and saw Jake waving.

My spirits shot up and suddenly, buffa-human or no buffa-human, I was glad to be reunited with my friends.

No matter what happened in the end.

CHAPTER 17

"How could it have survived that fall?" Marco asked, glancing pointedly at the buffa-human and giving me a hard look.

"It was pretty bad," I admitted, avoiding his cool gaze. "It saw me demorph, though and mimicked me. I guess that saved it." Sure. I *guessed*. How about I knew?

"I just can't get right with this," Rachel said. "I mean, it's bad enough that we have this mutant thing following us around, but did it have to go and acquire someone we know? I know I'll never be able to look at Chapman again without freaking out. It's too weird."

The buffa-human had hunkered down at the edge of our circle. Its eyes were disturbingly blank, absent of human recognition and intelligence. It was watching us, though, and warily sniffing the air. It was listening, too, gauging the tones of our communication and on the alert for any type of alarm call. A buffalo in human skin.

It was unnerving.

"It's gross," Marco said, looking away.

<It is dangerous,> Ax looked at me with his main eyes while the ones on stalks surveyed the area.

"Yeah," Jake said, weakly smiling at me as I sat down on the rocks next to him, keeping the blue box between us. "Glad you made it."

"Me, too," I said, smiling back, faintly. "That drop-off was pretty bad."

"Guhhhhd," the buffa-human said, tensing when all heads swiveled in its direction. "Guhhhd?"

"No, not good, *bad*," Marco said, scowling.

The buffa-human frowned and pressed its lips together. "Baaaaadd?"

"I'm teaching my assistant principal to talk," Marco said. "Is this whacked or what?"

<It's not Chapman,> Tobias said. <Remember that. It's not Chapman.>

<It's learning,> I said, absently brushing a black ant from the morphing cube. It hit the ground and ran up my leg.

"No, it's not, Cassie. It's only mimicking,"

93

Rachel insisted, shaking her head. "Don't make this more than it is. It should have died a long time ago."

"She's right," Marco said, giving me a knowing look. "You didn't do it any favors by keeping it alive, Cassie. Now one of us is going to have to . . ."

There was an uncomfortable pause.

"Well," Jake said, rising. "I think we'd better get moving again. The Yeerks are going to find us, no question about that, but we want to be in place when it happens."

"Mee-meep," Marco said, jumping up. "Anvil time."

I rose slowly. The buffa-human did, too.

"You have to get it to morph back to buffalo," Jake said, avoiding my eyes. "It's probably safest that way. The rest of us will head out. We'll move slow enough for you to catch up, Cassie."

And the buffalo? I wanted to ask. What about it? Am I supposed to lead it off another cliff, or out into the dangerous undertow and abandon it? What was I supposed to do with this poor, mutated animal that never should have existed? And why was I the one who was going to have to kill it?

But I didn't ask that last question because I knew what they would say.

And they were right, only . . .

I turned away as the others began their morphs.

"Ready?" I said in a low voice to the buffa-human, blocking his view of the others.

It cocked its head. "Guuuuhhhdd."

"Yes, you're good," I whispered, closing my eyes and concentrating on the buffalo's powerful DNA. "Now, pay attention."

I felt the changes begin. The usual. Bones grinding, contorting, wrenching backward and forward, stretching and disappearing. The feeling that your entire body is shot full of Novocain, so you're aware of the impossible crunches and gurgles, but you don't actually feel them.

I opened my eyes and saw the buffa-human finishing its morph. Thick horns were crawling out of the center of its massive head, slithering down past its tufted ears, and curving back up with deadly accuracy.

SPRROOT!

Its tail sprouted and it flicked it.

<Good,> I told him in thought-speak, watching his ears flick and twist, disturbed at the sound that made no sound outside his head.

Thwok thwok thwok!

Jake picked up the blue box and held it tight in his jaws. <Cassie?>

I moved behind a huge clump of bushes,

where the buffalo couldn't see me. Demorphed and remorphed into a wolf.

I felt my teeth shifting in my gums, sprouting into long, gleaming fangs. Felt my body stretch and grow sleek with powerful muscles. Felt the thick ruff of fur ring my neck and ripple across my body.

Thick pads bulged and hardened on my hands and feet.

My skull cracked and remolded, expanding into a canine muzzle.

<Ready?> Jake called impatiently.

<Ready,> I said, as soon as the morph was finished.

<Then let's —> Rachel began.

<Do it!> Marco said in his best "superhero voice."

The air stirred as the others raced out of the clearing.

I smelled the buffalo's confusion. Heard the dull clop of its hooves against rock as it hurried after them, snorting and calling, puzzled at being left behind.

And suddenly, I was overcome. Fear. Frustration. Panic. Exhaustion.

Why had this happened! To us? To this poor creature?

I didn't know and would never know. And I was tired of not having the answers.

With a whimper I bolted into the woods after the others. Bulleted past the lumbering buffalo. Ignored its plaintive calls.

Ran and ran and ran until the faint scent of the salty ocean filled my nostrils. Ran until the buffalo's cries had faded to whispers, replaced by the dull, insistent throbbing of a distant, but approaching helicopter.

CHAPTER 18

I could hear the others padding swiftly through the woods in front of me and the faint crashing of the surf against the shoreline.

I didn't want to think about the buffalo lost somewhere behind me.

<There's a helicopter doing a zigzag search back over the ravine,> Tobias called. <It's definitely tracking us, Jake. Coming fast!>

<Time for Operation Anvil to kick in,> Jake said.

Thwok thwok thwok!

The helicopter was getting closer.

The plan had to work.

I started to demorph.

Something was moving in front of me.

"Uhhh!" I backed up.

Gaped at the ground in front of me.

Something was growing. Fast!

Black. Bulging. Three inches. Eight inches.
Now it was a foot high.

It was an ant, antennae waving and pincers
snapping.

And it was getting bigger.

Two feet high. And counting.

Demorph, I thought frantically, trying to
scrabble away from the ant's sharp, snapping
pincers. *Demorph!*

And the ant was still growing, its arms
and legs waving, hair sprouting from its bulby
head —

Hair?

The tips of its top pair of legs swelled and fingers erupted.

Its segmented body melted and ran together,
reshaping into a sturdy, human form.

Wide, human eyes popped out of its head,
flanking a strong, familiar-looking nose.

SCHWIPP! SCHWIPP!

Its pincers were jerked halfway back into its
head, leaving the lethal tips spasming, and in between them, in some horrible, terrifying morph-

ing disaster, the ant's face split vertically and lips formed.

Opened wide in a silent scream as gleaming, white teeth erupted from the pink gums.

Please, no.

I was gazing at myself.

CHAPTER 19

Somehow, and I don't know how, maybe through my own human survival instinct, I finished demorphing, shooting back up to my full height. Now I was looking the ant-Cassie square in the eye.

It was horrible. Terrible.

It writhed and jerked, body parts melting then hardening from ant to human and back.

Antennae burst from its human skull, were sucked back in, then shot out again.

It looked around, eyes bulging with panic, and opened its mouth in a scream straight out of my worst nightmares.

"AAAAAARRRRGGGGHHH!" Raw torment.

I staggered back, clapped my hands over my ears, tried to shut out the unearthly shrieks.

How had this happened? Where had this second abomination come from? How could an ant have gained the power to morph!

There was only one way.

The blue box. The ant must have touched it.

Yes, it had, back when we had been resting on the rocks. The ant had been crawling on the box and I'd flicked it off. Then it had crawled up my leg. It must have acquired me without having any idea of what it was doing.

I glanced back at it, watching it scream and writhe like it was in mortal agony.

Why would it be in pain? Morphing didn't hurt . . .

And then the memories I had of being an ant resurfaced and I knew why the ant-Cassie was so terrified. For the same reason, except in reverse, that I never wanted to morph an ant again.

They were all part of a collective. Mindless, soulless beings without wills or thoughts of their own.

When the ant had morphed to human it had become an individual with the freedom to choose. With free will. The human brain, with all its diversity and innate curiosity, must be completely overwhelming it.

Logically, I knew that. Emotionally, I was watching myself twist and squirm and double over in agony and I couldn't take it.

"Stop it!" I shouted.

Bad move.

It reared up and focused on me.

And then its pincers sprouted full-length on either side of its human mouth, and it attacked.

I stood, frozen in horror as it flung itself at me, stumbling awkwardly on two legs.

Pincers snapping. Grazing my leg.

The pain woke me up.

"No!" I screamed, darting sideways.

The ant moved with me, waving its arms, smacking and slapping at me.

"No! No!" I sobbed. I tried to run, to get away from this hideous mutation of me, from this insanity. But I tripped over a branch and went down hard on my back.

Instantly, the ant sprang. Landed on top of me.

Reared up, pincers opening and closing. Arms melting back into spindly ant legs, then remorphing into human ones. Blocking my frantic punches and kicks. Growing shiny white teeth in a wide, wet, keening mouth and then shifting back into ant mandible.

The pincers clamped down on my arm. Squeezed hard. Harder.

It was going to snap my arm and the pain was unbearable.

"NO!!" I screamed.

That's when I heard the now-familiar bellow.

The ant-Cassie jerked upright, dragging me with it.

"Here! Here!" I cried hoarsely, kicking at the ant as the buffalo charged into sight.

Thwok thwok thwok!

The buffalo lifted its head and scented the air. Tossed its horns.

"EEEEEEEE!" the ant-Cassie screamed, dropping me and wheeling to face it.

Crying, cradling my torn and bloody arm, I dragged myself out of the way.

The ant-Cassie, antennae waving madly and pincers snapping like the jaws of a steel trap, ran crazily at the buffalo.

THUNK!

The buffalo twisted its horns and gored it right through the stomach.

"EEEEEAAAHHH!" it screamed, arching backward, beating on the buffalo's head with its fists and finally, with a wet, popping sound, pulling itself free.

It staggered backward, clutching its bloody abdomen, pincers snapping weakly and human mouth opening and closing.

I was watching myself die. Not as a human or an animal, but as a terrifyingly mindless drone.

A nightmare.

I threw up in the bushes. Sat up and wiped my mouth.

The buffalo cried out, in triumph.

But it wasn't really triumph, because instead of dying the ant-Cassie was shrinking. Demorphing into a vile jumble of ant and human parts. Growing tinier and tinier.

"No," I croaked.

I staggered over. Stomped the ground. Stamped and crushed everything and everywhere.

Slammed my bare feet down again and again and again until it had to be dead because such a hideous abomination could never, ever be allowed to live.

Thwok thwok thwok!

The helicopter was closing in, drawn, undoubtedly by all the morphing energy.

I had to go right now or our plan would be ruined.

The buffalo had relaxed a little and was eating the sparse grass at the edge of the woods.

I stepped beneath a tree. Focused on the osprey DNA.

Instantly, I was yanked down toward the ground, falling at a dizzying rate of speed and then stopping short like a runaway elevator slamming into its next floor.

A lacy, dappled pattern etched across my skin and rose into feathers.

My face stretched out, pursing my lips into a beak and hardening like quick-drying cement. My eyes crawled to either side of it and my vision sharpened.

My bones ground and hollowed out.

Tail feathers sprouted.

The morph was completed.

I flapped my powerful wings and hopped up onto a rock.

The buffalo looked at me, puzzled and uncertain again.

I looked back, not knowing what to say or do.

It gave a questioning snort and stepped closer.

THWOK THWOK THWOK!

<I have to go now,> I said, knowing it couldn't understand me. <Thank you for saving my life.>

The buffalo's ears twitched.

And then I knew what to say.

<You are good,> I said softly.

Its ears came forward and it made a soft, almost friendly sound.

The helicopter buzzed into sight.

TSEEEEEW!

And then the Dracon beam blew up the buffalo.

CHAPTER 20

I shot out of the trees with dozens of other frightened, fleeing birds, flapping my powerful wings and fighting frantically for altitude against the helicopter's fierce downwash.

The helicopter circled the clearing where smoking pieces of the buffalo lay.

They had killed it and yeah, okay, they'd saved me from having to come back and do it myself.

But that still didn't stop the feelings. Not at all.

That buffalo had trusted me and for reasons it didn't understand, maybe would never have been able to understand, I'd let it down.

Or maybe somewhere in its developing, learning human mind, it had understood.

I would never know.

I escaped the helicopter's swirling air currents and headed out over the ocean in the dull, gray half-light of the approaching dawn, fighting to go higher and higher.

Far below me, I could see five identical dolphins swimming out to sea.

And now, not so far below me, swooped a Bug fighter followed by the helicopter.

I was fighting to rise, flapping hard against the dead air. If Operation Anvil was going to work and we were going to destroy the Helmacron sensors aboard the ship aboard the helicopter, I had to be high enough to drop the anvil.

TSEEEW! TSEEEW!

The Yeerks were firing Dracon beams at the dolphins.

The dolphins dove, but I couldn't tell if they'd done it in time to avoid getting hit.

Higher, Cassie, higher, I told myself, struggling.

TSEEEW! TSEEEW!

<I'm hit!> Tobias cried faintly.

TSEEEW! TSEEEW!

The Bug fighter swooped and dipped, closing in, almost like it could smell blood.

<Dive! Dive!> Jake yelled.

The dolphins disappeared again.

They were deliberately drawing all the fire,

distracting the Bug fighter and the helicopter so I could put the plan into effect.

But was it going to work?

While the Bug fighter swooped and buzzed low over the ocean, the helicopter was hovering like a giant dragonfly in one spot — directly above where the dolphins were last seen.

In order for me to drop this anvil, I had to be directly above the helicopter. If it moved, the whole plan would be wrecked.

A helicopter could outrun an osprey, no contest.

But I couldn't think about that. If I did, I'd think even harder and see all the other things that could go wrong. And then I'd think about what would happen once everything did go wrong and I'd be lost.

The dolphins resurfaced farther out.

The helicopter moved again, hovering over them while the Bug fighter blasted away with the Dracon beams.

<Jake, can you hear me?> I shouted, flapping and straining for altitude. <Don't move anymore! Stay where you are!>

<Hurry, Cassie,> came his faint reply. <Tobias and Marco are hit and there's a lot of blood in the water!>

My heart skipped a beat.

Blood meant sharks and they were the last thing we needed right now.

<I'm going to drop the anvil, Jake!> I yelled back, leveling off high above the helicopter. <Just stay where you are! If you guys move then I'm going to miss the helicopter!>

His answer was too faint to hear.

TSEEEW! TSEEEW!

The dolphins surfaced and dove again.

I followed it until I was once again directly overhead.

TSEEEW! TSEEEW!

<. . . losing a lot of blood . . .>

<. . . Cassie . . .>

The thought-speak was faint, fragmented, and broken.

I'd just have to risk it. Risk it all on this one, insane plan modeled after an old cartoon I didn't even like.

And I'd have to do it fast because still distant but speeding closer and closing the gap, came the sharks.

So there, way up in the vast, cloudless sky over the enormous ocean, above a Bug fighter teeming with Yeerks and a helicopter with lethal, slicing rotor blades and a deadly, sucking engine intake, I demorphed.

Without a net.

CHAPTER 21

The demorph should have been smooth.

I should have been able to hold on to my wings until the last possible minute. But I was completely burnt out.

The demorph went weird and instead of becoming an osprey-sized Cassie with wings, I lost the wings first and began plummeting down through the air, streaming and rolling head over heels, desperately trying to finish the demorph.

I was rushing down, the wind sharp and hard, making me gasp for air.

Concentrate!

The feathers faded and skin spread across my body. I grew in one overwhelming surge to human size. My beak shriveled and disappeared. Arms and legs shot out.

Frantically, I focused on the humpback whale DNA coursing through my bloodstream.

Yes, that was our plan. That was it.

I'd morph to a gigantic whale — the anvil — and drop out of the sky down onto the helicopter, crushing it and sending it crashing down into the sea. It was sort of like an idea we'd used once before — and it had worked then. I was hoping it would work again.

And hopefully, I wouldn't get sliced to ribbons in the process.

Or trap the other Animorphs beneath the wreckage.

But I was falling too fast, I could feel it. Not even my expanding mass could slow me down.

TSEEEW! TSEEEW!

I was bloating, bulging up and out. I was as big as a minivan but it wasn't big enough.

The skin on the top of my head crawled and opened into a blowhole.

My bones crunched, ground, and knitted into a small but stretching whale skeleton. My arms flattened into flippers.

The roar of the chopper was numbing my brain.

I could feel the air trembling each time the slicing blades revolved.

I wasn't going to make it!

I wasn't big enough and I wasn't going to be by the time I hit the helicopter.

I was going to be sliced up like deli lunch-meat and flung far and wide across the ocean to feed the sharks.

That's when a movement caught my eye.

At first I couldn't tell what it was.

Then I realized it was just one of a few of the gulls frightened by the helicopter's downwash.

And then the helicopter pilot below me glanced up. His eyes bulged and with one swift jerk, he yanked the helicopter out from under me.

I was going to miss him! Even at my ballooning rate I was still going to miss him!

The mission had failed!

I'd failed.

TSEEEW! TSEEEW!

The Bug fighter swooped in below the helicopter, blasting the wounded, surfacing dolphins again and again.

It was all over now.

Within seconds the others would be dead. If the Bug fighter didn't get them, then I'd end up crushing them to death. The Yeerks would have the morphing cube and the human race would be finished.

SCHWOCK!

114

I couldn't believe it.

One of the gulls had been sucked into the helicopter's powerful, jet engine intake like a hairball into a vacuum hose.

KA-BOOOOM!

The helicopter exploded in a raging ball of fire.

The impact hit me like a warp-speed eighteen-wheeler. Sledgehammered the air from my lungs. Stunned me into shocked, deafened numbness.

Then came the scorching heat from the explosion, and the agony.

I was flung away from the burning wreckage, down toward the ocean.

And the last thing I thought in the millisecond before it all went black was, *After all this, all it took was one poor seagull . . .*

CHAPTER 22

<C assie? Cassie? Can you hear me?> Jake said urgently.

"No," I mumbled, shaking my head and immediately breathing in a noseful of salt water. "Gak. Ugh." I coughed, floundered, and when I couldn't get a handhold, panic set in. My eyes popped open.

The first thing I saw was a dolphin with the blue box in its mouth.

The second thing was miles of choppy, gray water with a far-off outline of land.

No wonder I was wet, shivering, and pruny. I was human again, and floating on my back in the middle of the ocean, surrounded by dolphins who were gently supporting me with their snouts and nudging me along toward the shore.

My brain kicked in and it all came back, the buffalo, the ant-Cassie, and the humongous, teeth-rattling explosion. Panicking, I started to thrash and sank like a stone.

<Easy,> Rachel said, dipping down beneath me and pushing me back up to the surface. <What're you trying to do, drown yourself? It's all over now. We're okay.>

"How?" I managed to croak, still hacking up bitter salt water and trying to get control of my normal, human brain long enough to calm the billowing fear. I mean, let's face it, the ocean was vast, deep and had swallowed hundreds, no thousands of better swimmers than me. Not to mention being home to sharks.

So, of course, I mentioned this fact.

<Oh, them. You missed all the fireworks, Cassie,> Marco said, swimming circles around us. <One minute we're watching this whale the size of a FedEx truck dropping out of the sky and we're thinking, *Uh-oh, she's not big enough to take down that helicopter and live through it* —>

<You weren't thinking it, you were screaming it,> Rachel said sweetly.

<Screeching like a bad set of brakes,> Jake teased.

<Emitting a loud and continual series of high-pitched shrieks similar to an unauthorized entry into a Dome ship air lock,> Ax added.

Silence.

<Well, it was an accurate comparison,> Ax said defensively.

<Yeah.> Marco giggled. <But it sure wasn't funny, Ax-man,> he said, poking his sleek head up out of the water and giving one of those crazy, Flipperesque cackles.

<Your humor is highly overrated,> Ax muttered.

<It certainly is when Marco uses it,> Jake said.

<Anyway,> Marco said loudly, <here you are, falling through the sky, and all of a sudden BOOM — >

"A gull got sucked into the helicopter's engine. But that was nothing compared to the ant-Cassie that almost killed me back in the woods with its pincers." I stopped. "The buffalo saved my life."

<You had an aunt who tried to kill you with her pincers?> Rachel said, giving me a playful nudge. <Boy, and I thought Tobias's family was bad.>

"Not that kind of an ant," I said crossly.

<I know,> Rachel said. <Geez, where's your sense of humor?>

<Probably caught back in the Dome ship's air lock with Ax's,> Marco muttered.

I zoned out for a minute while they bantered back and forth, thinking of the buffalo and how bravely it had fought side by side with us. Had it done it because the human DNA in his veins had stirred and somehow linked us together? Or had it simply been following his buffalo instincts and done whatever he had to do to protect its adopted herd? Or had it been a little of both?

I'd never know for sure, but I did understand the buffalo better. Its survival and protective instincts were strong, fiercely and powerfully strong, and in that way, we were the same. How many times had my friends and I fought to protect our species from the Yeerk invasion? And how many times would the buffalo fight to protect its own from other predators, including humans?

<Hey, you'd yell, too, if sharks were eyeing you up like sushi,> Marco retorted.

<We were all in the water, remember?> Rachel purred.

<But you weren't pumping out blood like a fire hydrant,> Marco said.

"The helicopter blew up," I interrupted, teeth chattering. "The Helmacron sensors are destroyed, right?"

<Well, we're pretty sure they are,> Jake said slowly.

"So, you're *pretty* sure the sensors are DOA," I said. *Say yes, Jake,* I begged silently. *Say yes.*

119

Please don't tell me the whole mission has been in vain. That I had to confront my physical self as an ant, as a mutant, a thing . . .

<Yeah,> Jake said. <We're ninety-nine percent sure, Cassie.>

Oh, great. That left a one percent wild card.

<Cassie, you did great, > Jake said, in private thought-speak. <And I have to tell you, when I saw you heading for that chopper's blades, well, Marco wasn't the only one freaking out. We moved out of the way and dove deep when you all came down, but when you hit the water you were burned pretty bad —>

I closed my eyes, remembering the searing pain and the stench of sizzling whale blubber.

<— and we were going crazy trying to get you to demorph. You were only, like, half-conscious but I guess that was enough. I'm glad,> he said simply.

"Me, too," I said.

Survival instincts. Funny, how our own genetic programming would automatically kick in when our logical, reasoning, conscious human brains weren't around to jam them up.

<Me, too, what?> Tobias asked.

<It's *private* thought-speak, Bird-boy,> Marco said. <Jake's getting all Dharma and Greg on us with Cassie.>

I laughed but I was shivering so it came out ratchety and harsh. I wasn't embarrassed that

120

Marco had guessed what was going on. Jake and I like each other a lot and that's no secret.

<Cassie, why don't you morph to dolphin and let's all get out of here,> Jake said, noticing my quaking. <I'm done with this day at the beach. How about you guys?>

<Your wish is my command, Prince Jake,> Marco said.

<Then I wish you'd be quiet,> Jake drawled.

<Ha-ha!> Ax said. <Ha!>

We all looked at him, amazed.

<That was, I believe, the appropriate response to human humor, correct?> he said calmly, then dove and, within seconds, had powered his sleek dolphin's body up out of the water and high into the air.

<I quit,> Marco said, groaning. <If Ax is gonna "ha-ha" after all of Jake's feeble jokes from now on, I swear I quit.>

But he wouldn't and we knew it.

None of us would.

No matter how bad the odds.

Or the humor.

#40 The Other

It was just a blue blur moving across the screen. Not much more than that. A small piece of video tape taken with an unsteady hand in terrible light conditions.

But it was enough.

My fool-proof danger alarm went off. Loud.

"Could this be proof positive of the existence of the magical unicorn of medieval lore?" the host intoned. "Or could this strange blue creature be the mighty centaur of Greek mythology? Let's take another look."

I hit the power button and the screen went gray.

One look had been more than enough.

The image was blurred but unmistakable.

Andalite.

I scaled the stairs to my bedroom two at a time.

This was bad. Really bad. A serious breach in security. The beginning of our end . . .

A good bazillion citizens of the United States of America, and who knew how many people in how many other countries had just gotten their first glimpse of a bona-fide alien.

Eighty, maybe ninety percent of those viewers would be excited for about thirty seconds — at least until the next silly monster after the next silly commercial.

Ten, maybe twenty percent of those viewers would recognize the blue blur for what it was. Not a unicorn or a centaur.

An Andalite. Here. On Earth.

And it could only be Ax.

Okay, Visser Three and every other Yeerk with a host knew of the "Andalite bandits." The ones who formed the small but unrelenting resistance to the Yeerks' movement.

But others — humans not controlled by Yeerks — didn't know. And they couldn't. Shouldn't. It was too dangerous, too risky. Bad for Ax to be taken prisoner by the visser. Worse for him to be taken for study by the government.

Not everybody in "the agency" was as fair-minded as Scully or Mulder. Some were even Yeerks.

Ax would not be taken. I would make sure of that.

A thousand fears and anxieties ran through

my head, almost as quickly as I ran up the steps and into my room.

I had to get control. Focus. Maintain that focus.

I went to the bed. Arranged the pillows under the blankets to look like a sleeping kid. So my dad and my stepmother wouldn't know I was gone. Again.

I stripped down to my morphing suit. Tossed jeans, T-shirt, and sneakers into the pit that is my closet. Tore open the window. And began to morph.

The goal: rapid transportation.

PING! PING!

I winced. The beginning of talons, where my toes had been only a few seconds ago. I watched as the rest of my feet and ankles withered, shrunk, and suddenly became the bird's incredibly strong, gripping feet. Three long, fleshless talons facing front, one facing back.

No way those feet could support my thick human legs. I was going down.

THUMP!

I was definitely down. But I'd fallen on my back. I lifted my head and watched as my legs blackened and shriveled up into my body like two sticks of beef jerky being sucked up by a gnarly old cowboy.

Right then I vowed never ever to eat a Slim Jim again.

In spite of what you might think, morphing doesn't hurt. It's just disgusting.

But still, I watched. As if I could hurry the process by witnessing it. Fingers — curling into my palm. Tanned human flesh lightening to gray and then disappearing under a flat, three-dimensional tattoo of feathers. Then arms sprouting feathers in a fury. At the same time, arm bones shrinking, hollowing, reshaping. Becoming wings.

My mouth and nose melded together, hardened to form a curved and deadly beak.

Internal organs? I felt approximately twenty-five feet of human intestines smoosh and squish down to a bird's tiny digestive tract. My slow and steady human heart surged into the manic, pulsing heart of the bird of prey.

No longer human. No longer tall enough to see the unopened notebooks scattered over the desk. The handful of empty bubble gum wrappers I should probably throw away. Close enough to the carpet to see boulders of cookie crumbs and single strands of curly poodle hair. Ugh.

I was an osprey. The animal that had become one of my earliest morphs. Not a bird with the greatest night vision but vision a heck of a lot better than a human's. Vision good enough to get me where I was going.

Ax's scoop.

I hopped up onto the windowsill. Glanced sharply around with beady eyes to be certain the house wasn't being watched. And flapped into the night air.

Ax was at "home."

And he had company perched on a nearby branch.

<Tobias!>

<What brings a guy like you to a place like this?>

<Nothing good.> I flared my wings and landed on the soft grass and dirt. Started demorphing.

<When is it ever good when one of us just shows up, all unexpected?> he added.

I didn't answer. Tobias has been big on rhetorical questions lately.

Besides, at the moment, I didn't have any of what Ax would call "mouth parts."

But I did have eyes. Ax's TV was on. But not on the station I'd been watching.

As soon as my lips were formed I looked directly at Tobias. Then at Ax. "Our buddy Ax here is a star," I said brightly, brushing dried-out pine needles off my bike shorts, wincing when a sharp stone bit into my tender human foot.

I told them what I'd seen. When I'd finished, there was silence.

It was Tobias who spoke first. <Well, Ax?> His thought-speak was hoarse. Almost anxious. <Is it possible?>

Ax hesitated. Turned his main stalk eyes to look behind him, toward the deeper woods.

<Anything is possible,> he said.

That was not what I wanted to hear.

<I guess we need to get a copy of that episode.>

"D'ya think? Really?" I said, rolling my eyes. "Okay. Listen. We don't have time to wait around for the rerun or to send a check to the station in order to buy a copy. We just can't risk waiting."

<That's true.> Ax said as he stepped to his television set-up. <But we don't have to wait.>

"Did I miss something? Cause I'm definitely not understanding."

<Ax tapes everything,> Tobias explained. <On every channel. He's set up a CD-ROM thing to the VCR — or something like that. Anyway, it works.>

<Marco, I believe this is what you're looking for.>

Ax stepped back from his small pile of mechanics. With a remote, he fast-forwarded through the thirty minute show until he reached the segment.

All twenty seconds of it.

Ax froze the final frame.

More silence. This time, I broke it.

"Is it you, Ax?"

Ax briefly focused all four eyes on the screen before sweeping those on stalks around the perimeter of the scoop. Wary now.

<I cannot tell from that angle.>

<Play it back in slow motion,> Tobias suggested. <Frame by frame.>

Ax did. To me it still didn't make any difference.

It could have been Ax.

It could have been any Andalite.

But the only other Andalite we knew of on Earth was Visser Three. No way would he ever be careless enough to allow himself to be caught on film. Besides, he was never without a phalanx of bodyguards.

Unless . . . unless he *wanted* to be seen by thousands of couch potatoes. But why?

"Ax-man. Is there any way to fine tune the image?" I asked.

<No. I cannot clear the resolution on a nonoriginal piece of film or video.>

Tobias swooped off his perch and landed, gracefully, a few feet from the television screen.

<You don't have to,> he said. <It's not Ax.>

"So it's the visser," I said. "Well, that's a little beyond weird."

<No. Not the visser.> Tobias turned his incredibly intense hawk eyes on us. <Kids, I think we've just discovered another Andalite.>

Ax pulled his shoulders back. <Is it . . .>

<It's not Estrid. Sorry, Ax. Not Arbat, either.>

"Alrighty then. Who?"

<This guy's new. And he's got one real obvious distinguishing feature. He's got only half a tail.>

<A *vecol*!> There was disbelief in Ax's voice. Something else, too. More than his normal, well, arrogant tone. It sounded like disgust.

"Excuse me?" I asked.

<He is disabled. A cripple,> Ax answered coldly. <And his presence here will obviously be a problem.>

"Yeah," I agreed, looking back to the hazy image on the screen. "The Yeerks get a hold of him, they've got another morphing Andalite on the team. Not good."

<No. The Yeerks would have no use for his *body*. He is completely useless as a host.> Ax waved his frail hand in a dismissing motion. <Without a tail blade he cannot fight. And it is obvious this *vecol* is incapable of morphing or he would have restored his tail from his own healthy DNA.>

"So, Ax, how do you really, *really* feel about this guy? Let me take a wild guess." It sounded nasty. I meant it to.

<Marco.> Tobias. <Seems to me this, uh, guy, could be useful to the Yeerks in another way. He's got to have information the visser wants.>

"Which means wherever he is, we get to him first. Unless we're too late. Which I'm not even going to think about."

<Right,> Tobias agreed. <Best case scenario, he becomes an ally.>

Ax made a sound that was way close to a snort. <A *vecol* as an ally? Marco, was that meant to be humorous? Because it wasn't.>

I grinned. Folded my arms across my chest. "No, Ax. It wasn't meant to be 'humorous.' What's with you? What's your problem with this guy?"

Tobias interrupted. <Let's get going. We're going to need to talk to Jake and the others. We can deal with this other stuff later.>

I took a deep breath. Gave my hair a good yank, straight up. Spoke.

"Yeah. It's time to find us an Andalite. Oh," I said, looking blandly at Ax. "Let's not forget one other possibility here. In spite of the famous-throughout-the-galaxy Andalite honor, this guy could, as we know, quite possibly be a traitor. The whole video-tape thing might be a trap for us unsuspecting, big-hearted humans, who respond to creatures less fortunate than us with empathy and kindness."

<That is true,> Ax said, while staring back at me with his main eyes. <It might very well be a trap.>

ANIMORPHS®

K. A. Applegate

Everyone thought Visser Three and Ax were the only Andalites on Earth. Until now. An Andalite has been discovered on home video and shown on TV. Will he join the Animorphs in conquering the Yeerks? Or is he really part of a cunning trap to destroy the Animorphs?

ANIMORPHS #40: THE OTHER

Coming to bookstores this MARCH!

Visit the Web site at: www.scholastic.com/animorphs

Step Inside the World of

www.scholastic.com/animorphs

The official website

Up-to-the-minute info
on the Animorphs!

Sneak previews
of books and
TV episodes!

Contests!

Fun downloads
and games!

Messages from
K.A. Applegate

See what other fans
are saying on the Forum!

It'll change the way you see things.